SYSTEMA PARADOXA

ACCOUNTS OF CRYPTOZOOLOGICAL IMPORT

VOLUME 20
THE BILLABONG TRAIL
A TALE OF THE BUNYIP

AS ACCOUNTED BY JAMES CHAMBERS

NEOPARADOXA
Pennsville, NJ
2024

PUBLISHED BY
NeoParadoxa
A division of eSpec Books
PO Box 242
Pennsville, NJ 08070
www.especbooks.com

ISBN: 978-1-956463-47-7
ISBN (ebook): 978-1-956463-46-0

Interior Design: Danielle McPhail
www.sidhenadaire.com

Cover Art: Jason Whitley
Cover Design: Mike and Danielle McPhail, McP Digital Graphics
Interior Illustration: Jason Whitley

Copyediting: Greg Schauer and John L. French

DEDICATION

FOR STEPHANIE

FOREWORD

An unexpected package arrived at my front door on a searing July morning.

I found it when I returned home from walking my dogs, our regular stroll shortened by treacherous heat and air thickened with haze drifting across the entire Northeast from Canadian wildfires. After sending the dogs inside, I retrieved the box, about the size of a cooler and heavy enough that my first attempt to lift it failed. With a change of footing and a better grip, I hefted it into my house and dropped it on the kitchen table. It bore no address, no postage, no shipping labels, no indications of who'd sent it or how it had landed on my porch.

A blank cardboard enigma.

I hurried to the window and checked the street for a delivery van or other vehicle but found it empty. I stepped back outside onto the front porch and listened. Bird calls, insect buzzes, my neighbors' houses still and quiet. I hadn't walked the dogs far before turning back. It seemed impossible a delivery man could've left the box without passing us or being heard, but we hadn't encountered a soul. The heat and smoke kept everyone indoors.

I ran my fingers along the single, smooth strip of packing tape that sealed the box until my nail snagged an edge and peeled it away. Within, a sheet of paper folded in three with my name handwritten on it lay atop a pile of notebooks, photo albums, folders stuffed with maps and papers, an overloaded manila envelope, stacks of paperclipped pages, a shoebox of compact discs and flash drives, and a cell phone. In clean, simple cursive, the letter read:

You'll know what to do with this, like you did so superbly with Devil in the Green.

I'll call you in one week.

Yours,

Benjamin Keep

After two years and no word, Benjamin Keep dropped back into my life.

Since publishing Devil in the Green, *an account of Ben's investigation into a series of mysterious and troubling incidents that occurred on the east end of Long Island, I'd experienced every extreme of the writer's life. Readers stalked me to learn more about Bigfoot, Men in Black, the Montauk Monster, and alternate dimensions, believing I'd withheld secrets from the book. Cryptozoologists and paranormal researchers crusaded against me for the "hoax" I'd perpetrated. People pitched me to write books about their own experience with cryptids and other weird phenomena, despite having zero evidence. Literary critics panned* Devil in the Green *as "a cryptozoological potboiler" and lamented I hadn't shoehorned the Loch Ness Monster into the story too.*

I never wanted to write another book like Devil in the Green *— but as I sifted the cardboard cornucopia, I surmised that Ben expected me to do exactly that. I spent the rest of that day reading notebooks and yellowed newspaper clippings, typed and handwritten manuscript pages, listening to sound recordings on CDs and flash drives, tracing lines on tattered maps, and skimming old photos. A story emerged of a series of remarkable events spanning several decades and two continents. Much of it had occurred no more than fifty miles from my home, events Ben and his girlfriend, Annetta Maikels, had thoroughly investigated. After our last contact for* Devil in the Green, *I'd assumed they'd left Long Island, perhaps even New York, to escape being watched by the Men in Black and others, whose attention they'd attracted while documenting the truth about the Montauk Monster. Instead, they'd been hiding in plain sight, living on the down low only twenty or so miles west of me.*

The next several days brought little relief from the heat and haze, the perfect excuse to catalog the odd bounty in air-conditioned comfort. When the enclosed cell phone rang as promised one week later, I answered it prepared. Ben and I stayed on the phone only long enough for him to give me the address for a rundown Suffolk County diner, where, the next morning, I met him and Annetta Maikels, now his fiancé.

An outdated black sedan of no make or model I could identify caught my eye parked in the lot's last row. Tinted windows all around. A gold-on-black license plate. I'd seen a similar car once before, but Ben and Annetta claimed to have encountered them numerous times. Were the watchers observing Ben and Annetta or me? Was I reacting with paranoia? I told myself that coincidence presented a far more credible explanation. It almost always did.

It didn't help me shake off the sense of eyes tracking me, so invasive my skin crawled with it, as I entered the diner.

Over breakfast, Ben and Annetta convinced me of the veracity of their story if not the accuracy of their explanations and conclusions. That they believed it had all really happened the way they said, I had no doubt. I withheld judgment about the creature they encountered, though, partly to maintain objectivity and partly to defend my sanity. Likewise, I refrained from assessing their findings about how it all came to pass and what it revealed of the hidden workings of the universe.

Setting aside my reservations, I agreed to document the story as I'd done in Devil in the Green, *compiling their notes, transcribing recordings and interviews, and drafting Ben's reports into a narrative. To tell their story and, in part, the tragic story of Reginald Burgess. Ben permitted me again to share select materials with my publisher to assure them of the book's value and importance. You hold in your hands proof they found the evidence compelling.*

In my assessment, the value and importance of stories such as these motivates Ben and Annetta more than anything else. Incredible, unbelievable stories that confront our long-held notions about the nuts and bolts of the universe. Ben and Annetta have peeked behind the curtains of reality and believe humanity must ask hard questions, reject what our perceptions say at face value, dig deeper, and search longer until a glimmer of the truth emerges. We must fan that spark into a beacon. Lies come easy. They exist everywhere. We swim daily through lies like fish in the ocean. The world overflows with lies. We must work to obtain the truth which, as corny as it sounds, truly provides its own reward.

I've striven to capture Ben's voice and perspective, to withhold my comments and observations, to make this, as much as possible, Ben's story. All names have been changed. If you seek anyone described here, you won't find them. Nor would they talk to you if you did, at least not about anything written here. Where some people privy to these experiences might shout them to the heavens to soak up acclaim, Ben, Annetta, and the others involved understand the risk posed by the beings and forces at work — and the danger of too many people confronting them directly or in a manner perceived as threatening. The subtler our investigations and awareness of them, the less likely those forces will meddle with us. We must expose the truth by inches and degrees.

Whether or not you believe this tale doesn't concern me any more than it should concern you whether or not I believe it. The proof Ben provided and my conversations with him and Annetta convinced me to tell it. If it inspires you to seek answers to existence's larger mysteries, wonderful. If it merely entertains you for an afternoon or an evening, fine. Perhaps one day in the future, this book and Devil in the Green *will play some a part in achieving Ben's hope for humanity to look honestly and without preconceived notions into the universe we inhabit. I've done my best to recreate Ben's voice in the chapters that follow.*

James Chambers
Northport, NY

Chapter One

Annetta and I paddled over the river's surface and glided along a waterway carved 20,000 years ago when a glacier covered all of Long Island. Its discarded moraine formed the modern geography, leaving this fifteen-mile aquatic stretch, the Peconic River, the longest on the Island, flowing from Brookhaven to Flanders Bay, waters connecting ultimately to the vast Atlantic Ocean.

Hard to keep that sense of ancientness and prehistory in mind when houses, shopping centers, and industrial parks covered most of the Island, so jammed up that new development focused on building up rather than out, townhouses instead of single-family homes, office towers instead of commerce parks. Yet primordial pockets remained, protected by geography and conservation laws and, perhaps, by other forces. Modern progress made it ever more difficult, but anomalies and secrets still found ways to survive.

"Whoa, do you see that, Ben?"

Annetta set her paddle across her kayak and drifted.

Ahead of us, a great blue heron glided over a swath of spikerush grass, its wingspan almost six feet. A white perch dangled from its mouth. As it landed to eat its meal, the glassy river splashed and rippled. I raised my camera in its waterproof case and snapped a series of shots.

"Beautiful," I said.

Kayaking so early in the season, Annetta and I had the river to ourselves. The wildlife put itself on full display. We had already passed two white-tailed deer, a red fox, and three spotted turtles on the bank. The marshy waterway seemed like a quietly thriving world in full equilibrium with itself, devoid of the civilized chaos people inflicted upon each other on Long Island highways, in overcrowded big-box stores, even in their own backyards. I could almost believe the river hid something impossible and anomalous, a creature no one had yet identified—but it also struck me as a place that made it easy to see nonexistent things in the shadows. People accustomed to constant electric light and human contact sometimes found the slightest sense of isolation unnerving enough to open new synapses in their imagination.

The heron finished its meal then took to the wing and glided out of sight.

I lowered my camera. Annetta and I resumed paddling. We had set out west from Riverhead and planned to break for lunch at Peconic Lake, where the river widened to a larger body, before kayaking on to our target destination on the lake's other side. We journeyed the placid water in delicious quietude, soaking in the April sun and absorbing scenery lush with the peculiar green of nascent rebirth. Branches of red maple, white oak, and redbud trees bristled with buds. Yellow ribbons of wild forsythia, early to bloom, cut the green and brown with its brightness. Another hour passed before we reached a road-crossing. Annetta and I climbed out of our kayaks at the bank, then carried them up a steep ramp and across Dam Road to a matching ramp on the opposite side.

"Hey, why did the kayak cross the road?" I said.

Annetta grimaced then rolled her eyes.

Back in our kayaks, we set our sights on part of the bank along the Peconic River Campground. Annetta gazed downward, studying the water as we moved. When we reached the bank, we dragged our kayaks onto the ground and broke out our dry bags of food and drinks. Annetta sat on a shady rock, her face in a shaft of sunlight. Her beauty, as that perfect mix of light and shadow played across her deep brown skin, took my breath away. She caught me staring, smiled, then stuck out her tongue.

"This is pretty shallow water."

I eyed the smooth lake, the opposite shore not very distant, and nodded.

"Yeah, I think the deepest it gets is about six feet."

"I could see the bottom almost the whole way down from River-head." Annetta bit into her energy bar, chewed, then washed it down with a swig from her water bottle. "You know what I'm thinking, don't you?"

"Habitat."

"You got it. This is a dinghy versus a cargo ship as far as rivers go."

"So, how does a creature larger than a cow hide in such shallow water?" I bit into the buttered bagel I'd packed. Around a mouthful, I said, "It doesn't. I know it sounds like a copout, but it just means we have to look someplace we haven't yet. We still don't know what we're looking for. Does it prefer salt water or fresh water? This river lets out into an estuary that feeds a series of bays connected to the Atlantic Ocean. As far back as 1916, sharks have been known to swim up creeks and rivers in New Jersey. What if it's not a river monster we're hunting, but a sea monster?"

Annetta devoured the last of her energy bar and opened a second. "Or someone's horse got loose and went roaming down the river. There are plenty of stables in the area. The few reports really don't add up to much, Ben. I'm not complaining about spending the day kayaking with you, but I'm not seeing much of anything out here, love."

"Me neither. Doesn't mean it's not there. What if this thing is like our old friend Monty?"

Annetta frowned and sighed. "How many species capable of traveling between dimensions of reality do you think visit Long Island? How many even exist?"

"I have no idea. That's the point. We need to document it. No one else is looking into this stuff. If it's something totally different then we can either close the door on it or open a new one to investigate."

Annetta packed the wrappers from her energy bars into the dry bag, then stretched, giving me a glimpse of her bellybutton and smooth stomach as her shirt rode up. "Yeah, yeah, yeah, but what about the weirdos in the black cars?"

"We haven't seen one in months. Maybe they've lost interest in us."

"I sure hope so, but if we dig up the wrong thing, won't they get back on our case?"

I shrugged. Annetta raised an eyebrow.

Neither of us quite understood how the Men in Black worked or what they wanted. They first engaged with us during our investigation of the Montauk Monsters and the baffling and beyond merely anomalous appearance of several Bigfoots in the Long Island Pine Barrens. Neither of us knew what they might do if we set foot into their territory again. We agreed, though, any knowledge gained outweighed the risk—at least for now.

I finished the last of my bagel, gulped down some water, then we packed up, and cast off again. The remainder of our trip lasted another hour at a leisurely pace before we left the lake behind where the river resumed and reached the backyard of the house at 4 Estuary Drive.

The only house along that part of the river, it peeked out from overgrown boxwood, euonymus, and white pine that obscured it from the water. Tall weeds swamped the lawn between the back of the house and riverbank. Maples, oaks, and sycamores cast it in deep shade. I reached the bank first, pulled my kayak onshore, then steadied Annetta's while she hopped out. We stowed our life vests and paddles in them. I kept my camera slung around my neck.

The back of the house looked neglected but ordinary. Faded cedar shingles, windows grimed from weather and neglect, moss growing on the roof, and a few intrepid weeds sprouting from the gutters. We circled to the front, where damage from almost fifteen years ago remained unrepaired, boarded up by sheets of plywood now cracked and splitting from long exposure to rain, wind, and cold. Graffiti covered the boards, the names of people and rock bands, initials paired together inside hearts, crude drawings of faces, human anatomy, and animals.

I hefted a prybar out of my backpack. "Ready?"

Annetta nodded. "This is what we came for, isn't it?"

I jammed the prybar under an edge of the plywood sheet covering the front door and yanked.

CHAPTER TWO

From The East End Chronicle, *"Police Blotter," August 9, 1984*

Over the weekend, police briefly detained a group of local teens for underage drinking on the bank of the Peconic River. The teens approached a patrol car and reported a "river monster" had attacked them and dragged their picnic blanket into the water. They described the creature as larger than a cow and having a bulbous head. They claimed it rose from the river without warning then rushed them, snapping at them with a pair of tusks protruding from its lower jaw. Responding officers confiscated half a twelve-pack from the teens, then sent them home with a warning against underage drinking and making false reports.

Transcript of an audio recording, Benjamin Keep interviewing Joanna [last name redacted], one of the teenage witnesses to the mysterious river creature sighting reported on the Peconic River bank in 1984. Conducted in February 2023.

BK: Do you still reside in the vicinity of the Peconic River?

J: I live in Calverton now. Grew up in Riverhead, lived in Speonk for a while, before I settled down with my ex-husband. He really wanted the house, but the court gave it to me, so I've stayed there ever since to spite that sonofabitch.

BK: Is your ex one of the boys who was with you in 1984?

J: [laughter; coughing] Hell, no. That was Duane Sadowski. Dear old Daune did two things better than any other guy I ever knew: dance and kiss. Driving? Yeah, no. Wrapped his car around a telephone pole on

Route 25 in a storm six months after graduation. I cried my eyes out over old Duane. We'd never have lasted, but the poor boy deserved better than life gave him.

BK: What about the others with you that night, Oscar Feingold and Denise Rappaport?

J: Yeah? What about 'em? I haven't seen either since Reagan was in office. They moved to the city, never looked back. No idea where they are now. Their parents retired to Florida or North Carolina, I think.

BK: How often back then did you visit the location on the Peconic River where you saw the river creature?

J: Every weekend, pretty much. That was our place, you know? We weren't doing any harm. Kicking back and chilling out. We were only "underage" because they raised the age to 21 that year. One day we were legal, the next we weren't. Three weeks before, we weren't underage. So the cops didn't hassle us much for drinking as long as we didn't make trouble. And we didn't. We were never rowdy or loud.

BK: The night you saw the river creature, how much had you all had to drink?

J: A few beers a piece. We drank to relax, not get drunk. That was our make-out place. Booze wasn't the main reason we went there. It helped set the mood. [chuckling, then a long spate of coughing]

BK: How about you specifically? Were you drunk?

J: Nah, only buzzed. I was a lightweight back then. I went easy on the beer and never touched the hard stuff. I liked messing around with Duane, but I kept him in check, and that sweet old boy never tried to take advantage. Neither of us wanted to get in trouble. [sniffles, a sob] Excuse me, sorry. I haven't thought about those days or Duane in a long time. Anyway, it wasn't until I got married that I really learned how to drink. A husband will do that to you.

BK: What about controlled substances?

J: You mean drugs? I never got into that scene. It scared me. Oscar liked pot, and Denise usually joined him, but that's all. Nothing hard. Nothing to make us hallucinate, if that's what you're thinking. Duane didn't toke up because he had asthma. We were all pretty clear-headed that night.

BK: Were you doing anything differently? Did you bring any unusual food with you? Wear a new kind of perfume? Light candles or a fire?

J: Oh, god, how do I know? That was a long time ago. Longer than you've been alive, kid. We usually had some snacks with us. Oscar and Denise would smoke up then get the munchies. But that one night? No. Can't think of anything different. We were in our usual place, a little patch of the riverbank overhung by trees, like a natural tent, enough space for us to spread out, get ourselves some privacy. You couldn't see our spot from the path along the river, especially not at night, unless you knew it was there. It's still there like that today as far as I know. We never made a fire or anything because it might give us away. Most nights the moon lit things well enough. We liked it dark, anyway.

BK: When the thing came out of the water, what were you doing?

J: Necking. [laughter] I mean that's why we went there, right? Duane and I were pretty hot and heavy when Denise screamed. Oscar shouted. Then all of us saw it. Full moon that night lit up the river like a damn spotlight. The thing drifted into it, center stage. Cast a freaking shadow on us.

BK: Can you describe the creature for me?

J: Huge. Hairy. Scaly. Feathery. Like nothing else I ever saw before or since. It rose out of the river and stood there gawking at us. Its eyes shimmered like mirrors in the moonlight. Mirrors full of colors. Its head was jumbo-size and bobbled on its neck. Water dripped off it, splashing all over. It set one leg, or paw, or hand? I don't know. Some kind of mitt. Big is all I remember for sure. Planted it right on the bank. Gave a hissing sort of growl. I haven't thought about this in years. You know? I didn't forget, but I guess I wanted to. It terrified me. Its smell overpowered the stink of Oscar's joint. Not a bad odor. Just overwhelming. A little sweet too. It took another step toward us, put another paw on the bank. We screamed, grabbed what we could, and hauled ass. It didn't chase us, thank god. I looked back and watched it drag our blanket into the water with its paw. The moonlight lit up its face. A mouth full of teeth. Two long tusks jutting up from its bottom jaw. Then it swam away, kind of… snakelike? Like an otter, I guess.

BK: Did you see where it went?

J: Into the river. Then under it. Left behind bubbles and a little wake. Never saw our picnic blanket again.

BK: Did the creature resemble any particular animal?

J: You ever read that kids' book, *Where the Wild Things Are*? Those pictures are about as close as anything to how it looked. A mash-up of animals. Keep in mind, I didn't see it too great in the dark.

BK: How did you describe it to the police?

J: I didn't. Duane did. If you read the report, you got everything he said. He painted quite a picture for them. Not that they believed us. Laughed us off. Said we got drunk, spooked ourselves. Sniffed the weed odor clinging to Oscar. The only monsters were in our imaginations, they said. They sent us home. We didn't argue. We were lucky they didn't bust us for real. We didn't want to push our luck.

BK: You ever talk about the creature again after that night?

J: Hmmm, yeah, but not much. Oscar, Denise, Duane, and me got together the next day. Went back to the spot. It looked like it always did. I hoped we might see footprints or marks in the dirt, but I guess our picnic blanket padded the bank. None of us doubted what we saw. But what was the point of trying to convince anyone who hadn't been there to see for themselves? One weird night, but what it did mean? Not a damn thing. Life continued. We graduated. Oscar and Denise split. Duane drove himself into a tree. I married a caveman. You ask me, the only monsters that mattered to us were the ordinary ones. Duane went back to the bank at night a few times to see if it showed up again. It never did. He couldn't let it go. It haunted him. I've always wondered if that night had anything to do with his car crash. His state of mind wasn't the best when he died. We never resumed going there as a group, though. Our secret place felt tainted. Unsafe. It just didn't feel like *our* place after that. Once I lost my friends, I didn't see any reason to ever bring it up again. Not until you found me. Funny how well I remember it.

BK: I'm glad you do. It's very helpful.

J: Why do you care, anyway?

BK: I want to know the truth.

J: [laughter, coughing] Oh, uh-huh, the truth, sure, okay. About a monster I maybe saw when I was a kid? You must have better things to do with your time than that.

Chapter Three

Better things to do with my time.

I thought of a dozen without even trying, but none offered the elusive prize to which discovering the Peconic River monster might lead. The world knew plenty about the Loch Ness Monster in Scotland, Champ up in Lake Champlain, and Chessie down in the Chesapeake Bay. No one knew a damn thing about Long Island's mysterious river dweller—including that Long Island even had one. I sure didn't before the winter of 2023. Nor did I ever expect to find myself investigating it.

Long Island amounts to a speck on the globe. Although it runs almost 120 miles lengthwise, at its widest point—about 23 miles—a fit adult could walk a straight line from the Long Island Sound to the Atlantic Ocean in about six hours. Out of that, Brooklyn and Queens occupy a quarter of the Island with buildings and infrastructure on, under, and above nearly every square foot of it. Not a lot of hiding places for mystery monsters, unless alligators in the sewers or rat kings float your boat. Nassau, the next county over, offers only a few more cracks for odd creatures to slip through. Most homes there are four-car households. Constant human traffic creates a dearth of undisturbed habitat possibilities. The majority of the Island falls in Suffolk County, which contains the dwindling remnants of the Island's undeveloped land, its best beaches and parks, all of its significant preserves, including the Pine Barrens, and its longest river, the Peconic. It still struck me as incredible that the Island might house any kind of river beast. All the Island's rivers and lakes run shallow. Sea monsters off the coast seemed more its speed. Yet, the world harbors surprises in the most unusual places. Space and time don't always follow the rules we think they do. Places exist where they shouldn't. Time doesn't always move at a constant rate. In very special locations, realities overlap and occasionally commingle. Annetta and I had glimpsed the occult mechanics of the universe, sensed the purpose of those pockets of strangeness, and brushed shoulders with the beings that manage them. We came out of it with a different understanding of the universe… no, not an understanding, really, because all we genuinely understood was the universe didn't work the way we'd believed all our lives. Call it an awareness. We came away *aware* of the false reality in which we live. Imagine a hamster who believes its habitrail encompasses the sum of reality. Then some rotten kid carries it to the backyard and leaves it there in the open grass for the family cat to stalk. If that tiny hamster brain computes anything, it's that its universe is vaster, stranger, and more frightening than it ever imagined. But it still doesn't know what that all means.

No true knowledge, only an awareness.

Useful awareness, for sure, but the hamster, like me and Annetta, still lives in a grand deception. One that certain… people? Beings? Entities? I'm making up terms on the fly, so let's call them *cosmic park rangers* — park rangers in black suits, black hats, driving black cars, who watch the world to make sure we don't upset the balance or rat out the big reality grift.

As if anyone would believe us if we did.

It didn't matter what Annetta and I knew. It didn't matter we had evidence and witnesses. We didn't have the overwhelming "enough" to surmount modern cynicism. Not only did the rangers — the Men in Black — like to keep their secrets, but most of humanity seemed happy to oblige. Every report of weird phenomena, from alien abduction to Yetis in the Himalayas, meets the same reaction, doesn't it? Initial interest, maybe a little "this time it's different, maybe it's real" excitement, but then follows the doubt, the jokes, and the inevitable debunking. People shove it all into the junk drawer of social consciousness. No one really wants to know. If Bigfoot showed up in Times Square, the world would find a way to dismiss it as a hoax, a publicity stunt, or an ordinary man with a glandular condition. If they accepted Bigfoot for Bigfoot, even *worse*, they'd pity him, protect him, *humanize* him rather than take him as he is — and that's the real irony.

These things are *not* human.

Not the Montauk Monster, not the Men in Black, not Bigfoot, certainly not the twelve-legged spiders Annetta and I encountered and still spy now and then in the corner of a dirty window or the back of a dusty closet. That's what drew me back after swearing off all the weirdness and trying to fall back in step with the rest of the world.

I failed. Annetta fared no better.

After the Montauk Monster, we picked up where we left off, me with freelance photography and attempts at photojournalism, Annetta back to teaching biology at Brooklyn College. My career picked up. I shot assignments for a steady stable of clients around New York. Newspapers, magazines, ad agencies. Decent pay, easy hours, but of those three industries, one trafficked in lies with far more vigor than the other two. Hint, it wasn't advertising or magazines. Tough work if you value the truth. Annetta published in her field, attended conferences, lectured, became a tenured professor, even won some plum research grants. All in all, we'd done well. We enjoyed the normality that kind of life brought us because it allowed us to focus on each other and our life together.

We didn't talk much about our past.

Like Joanna said, *"What was the point of trying to convince anyone who hadn't been there to see for themselves?"*

We knew the truth. That should've been enough.

The funny thing about the truth, though? Once you knew it, you couldn't help how it took over your life and changed your perspective on everything else. You saw the world differently than everyone around you. They couldn't understand your needs, priorities, and values. That made us odd. Odd made us outcasts—and that made us lonely.

Annetta and I could take only so much before that outweighed our fear of the park rangers.

We'd hoped if we accepted their warning and left well enough alone… well, that didn't happen.

I never wanted to settle for "well enough." Neither did Annetta.

If we could prove one secret thing we knew, it would suffice. As if the universe itself sensed our restlessness, it dropped an opportunity in our laps in the form of a book Annetta brought home from work last December. The first words I read from it excited me as much as they terrified me:

"The natural world brims with mystery. For all the facts that human science secures, an infinite number of unknowns persist. Knowledge forms stepping-stones leading us closer to understanding how little we comprehend of Earth, the universe, and what lies outside the reach of our senses. Often, we must look back at our path and revise our perception of the stones along the

way. We see the path we thought we were on never existed, and we've been traveling a very different route the whole time. It shouldn't surprise us that creatures considered extinct, impossible, or mythical sometimes wander into our modern world to smash our smug perceptions of reality. It should surprise us it doesn't happen more often."

The night Annetta gave me the book, we sat at opposite ends of the sofa, our legs propped up and overlapped between us. I frowned at her after reading that passage. "What the hell is this?"

"You tell me." Annetta sipped red wine. "Real deal? Or Canal Street knock-off?"

I frowned, perused further before closing the book, keeping my place with my index finger. I studied the spine. Gold-stamped letters spelled: *Natura Occulta: My Adventures in the Hidden Realms*. Below them the author's last name: Burgess. I flipped to the copyright page next.

"It's self-published," I said. "Old school. Vanity press. Fancy and all, but seriously? Mr. Burgess paid a pretty penny to print these and probably wound up with a pallet of them in his basement because print-on-demand didn't exist in…" I glanced back at the copyright page. "…1982. Where'd you get it?"

"You remember Stuffy Jones in the botany department?"

"Yeah."

"His uncle died and left behind a bunch of books. Stuffy gave me a box of them he thought might interest me. This was in there."

"How is this different than inheriting someone's fifty-year-old collection of *Fate* magazines?"

"For one, everyone and their cousin interested in strange phenomena knows about *Fate*. No one knows about *Natura Occulta*. I spent four hours searching online and found not one mention. I called a dozen likely libraries and rare book dealers. No one's heard of it. Two, the guy who wrote it lived on Long Island. Half the stuff he claims to have experienced happened here, including out in the Pine Barrens."

I closed the book on my lap. Placing my hand on Annetta's leg, I squeezed it.

"I don't even know what to think about that."

"Don't think anything yet. Read the book *then* tell me what you think."

The leather cover gleamed in the living room's low light. The title topped the ancient symbol of the ouroboros, a snake devouring itself, below which appeared the author's full name: Reginald Burgess. I picked it up again, a thin volume printed on quality paper, a beautiful thing to touch that almost no one had ever held. I flipped it open back to the page where I'd left off and glimpsed Annetta over the cover.

"Go ahead, read," she said. "I'll wait."

I read. The whole thing. That night. Annetta waited, grading papers until I finished, and when I put the book down, I met her gaze eager for my reaction.

She leaned forward. "So?"

"Real deal," I said. "With a healthy dose of crackpot."

Annetta let out a squeal of delight. "I knew it! It's a sign, baby. We need to keep going. We've been on the wrong path all this time trying to hide and get back to 'normal' lives. This book found us. It's a sign from the universe."

"You heard the part about crackpot?" I said.

Annetta shook her head and grinned. "I distinctly heard 'real deal.' Let's focus on the positive. The universe wanted us to have it."

After sleeping on it, I agreed to investigate. We began our research, stepping onto the first stone in the path Burgess wrote about, and leading in a few months' time to plywood cracking away from cedar shingles as I wrenched the prybar and created an opening big enough to see a gloom-shrouded living room left wrecked and in disarray for more than a decade.

Chapter Four

From The East End Chronicle, *"Police Blotter," January 12, 2008*

Police reported a break-in at 4 Estuary Drive in Calverton. A man chasing his runaway dog on Sunday found damage to the unoccupied house there, the only one on the private road, and reported to police that the front door and window of the building were smashed inward. Investigators uncovered signs of vandalism and squatters. The house, which once belonged to Mr. Reginald Burgess, a native of Sydney, Australia, who moved to Calverton in 1982, has sat empty since Mr. Burgess disappeared four years ago. A botany professor, Mr. Burgess, was reported missing by colleagues at Sagtikos University in May 2004, where he taught and conducted research. He has no family in the U.S. Police found evidence of trespassers then secured the scene against weather and future break-ins.

Transcript of an audio recording, Benjamin Keep interviewing Garrett aka Gary [last name redacted], who discovered the damage and vandalism at 4 Estuary Drive in 2008. Conducted in February 2023.

BK: Why were you at the house at 4 Estuary Drive that night?

G: My damn dog ran off. I live over on Hill Street. My wife and I had adopted this dog, some mutt from who knows where, the sweetest thing ever — except when it came to walking on a leash or being fenced in. We named him Groovy — my wife's idea, not mine. I called him Houdini because that crazy pooch could find his way out of everything short of a locked room. We tried every type of harness and leash you can imagine. He found a way to squirm out of them all. He jumped right over any fence less than six-feet high. Could open our back storm door by jumping up and hitting the handle with his front paws. If he heard us say "walk," he'd disappear, and we'd find him in the driveway, waiting to go. I worried myself sick he'd get hit by a car on River Road, but he was a smart boy. He liked to go in bushes and yards more than the road, but from April to October we pulled enough ticks off him to fill a peanut butter jar, mostly dead ones, thanks to his FleaGard medicine.

BK: What happened that night you called the police to the house on Estuary Drive? He let himself out and went exploring?

G: Oh, no, no. Like I said, he never roamed far, and he never crossed River Road on his own, thank god. That night I took him for a long walk. The missus and I had a fight. Money, probably. That's about all we ever fight about. She likes to spend. I like to save. Got to the point where I knew one of us was going to say something we'd regret, so I took Houdini out to give myself time to cool off. Anyway, I got to walking, doing more thinking than watching. Next thing I know I'm across River Road. Houdini stops short, digs in, gets his haunches up, and the fur along his spine bristles. He growls, eyes something I couldn't see in the trees. It was dusk and visibility wasn't great. I figured he sniffed up a squirrel or a fox, something he might take for a threat. So, I'm standing there, staring into the dark, when he does this little hitchy dance, works the slack in the leash, then—BAM [a loud clap], I'm holding an empty leash, watching Houdini disappear down Estuary Road.

BK: You followed him?

G: Damn right! I loved that dog. So did the missus. He was a good boy except for his escape acts. Even that I couldn't hold against him too much. Who doesn't want to be free? But it wasn't safe for him to roam around that road. I jogged after him. Figured I'd catch up and find him waiting for me, his tongue hanging out, a great big dog grin on his goofy face.

BK: Did you?

G: Catch up to him? Oh, yeah. Find him happy and waiting? Nope. He was planted outside the front door of that house, growling, leaning on his back legs, the hair along his spine bristling up, completely intent on something inside, something he could sense but I couldn't see. The whole front wall of that house lay around us in rubble, a big gaping hole that looked like it had vomited out wood and sheetrock. Inside, totally dark. It gave me the shivers. Houdini's growling didn't reassure me.

BK: What did you see?

G: Do you mean did I see whatever had Houdini's hackles up? Maybe. I'm not sure when it comes to that. I saw something, though. Never again seen anything like it. But I've kept clear of that place, avoided that side of River Road ever since.

BK: What do you think it was you saw?

G: Some kind of animal. Big. Fast. That's about all I got. As I ran up after Houdini, this thing tore out from the smashed-up house, big enough that it knocked loose a bunch more boards and shingles on its way, trampled over the rubble, breaking glass and splitting wood, then it raced around the side of the house. Houdini chased it. I chased Houdini. I'd seen enough I near about shit my pants. Figured it was a bear. Now, yeah, I know there's no bears on Long Island, and it wasn't a bear, but I couldn't figure what else it might've been. Maybe it escaped from somewhere. How the hell could I know? It didn't matter at the moment. This thing and Houdini moved faster than me. They disappeared out of sight until I finally hoofed it around back. There's Houdini on the riverbank, barking, growling, spitting at a stream of ripples in the water, like he chased the thing and sent it running into the river. I get to Houdini, who calms right down when I put my hand on his withers. He lets me slip him right back into his harness. He wouldn't budge for a long time. Dug his feet in every time I tugged on his leash. Made me wait there while he watched the river. Finally, all the ripples disappeared. He turned and walked back around front of the house. I got my first good look at the damage then.

BK: What'd you find?

G: A lot of smashed in cedar, plywood, two-by-fours, sheetrock, and glass. I lit up inside with a flashlight I carried on walks to make sure cars would see me and Houdini. Found a couple of armchairs knocked over. A sofa with torn-up cushions like someone went at them with a garden claw. Empty food cans and beer bottles. Mostly used candles. Some newspapers. A beat-up suitcase. A kid's backpack that looked like SpongeBob SquarePants. Shreds of a sleeping bag. Part of it draped over someone's shoulders. That's when the awful stench hit me, and I saw what looked like bloodstains all over the place. Houdini stayed so close to me he bumped my legs every time I took a step. The whole scene started me thinking about the true-crime shows the missus watches all the time. That frightened me in a different way. I didn't want to go near whoever was under that scrap of sleeping bag, and Houdini tugged me away, so we went out front to the street, and I called the police.

BK: How long did you wait there?

G: Five, ten minutes. They hurried on over.

BK: Did you see anything else while you waited? Did anything happen?

G: Not a damn thing. That's one weird thing about that night it's hard for me to explain. While me and Houdini waited, everything seemed as still as a cemetery. No birds or critters. No insects humming. No sounds off the river. No cars passed by on River Road. We could've been the last two living creatures on Earth for those ten minutes. Then the police arrived, lights and sirens erasing that weird quiet. They got right to investigating. A couple officers escorted paramedics to the sleeping bag.

BK: What was in the sleeping bag?

G: That's the saddest part. It was the body of a migrant worker. Around here, they work the farms and vineyards, construction, restaurants, landscaping. Those who can't afford apartments make communities in out-of-the-way places. The woods or abandoned property. Cops figured this one found the house, watched it long enough to see no one lived there, then moved himself in. That place had been empty about four years by then. Has been ever since and still is. The guy who lived there, Reggie Burgundy or something? He vanished.

BK: Reginald Burgess.

G: Yeah, right. Burgess. His only family is in Australia, so someone there owns the place, but it seems they've got no interest in doing anything with it except letting it rot.

BK: What did the police tell you about the migrant?

G: One guy said I made the right call not touching anything. Might've disturbed evidence. Another cop laughed that off. Joked what they found might've upset my stomach. I guess he meant the body was so mangled it might've made me throw up. Hardee-har-har, right? One cop said something to another about the corpse being bit right through. That caught my attention, and the cop who said it? His face was pale as a sheet. Whatever happened, it was ugly. Didn't make any sense to me, though, so I stopped listening. I really didn't want all the gruesome details. Me and Houdini hung around long enough to give our statement, then they said we could go home. The missus was sore as hell over how long I'd been out. She was eager to make up with me and had been waiting longer than she liked. She cooled off when I explained what happened.

BK: Did you include what you saw run away from the house? The police report doesn't mention it.

G: I mentioned it at first, but when I saw the expression in the cop's face, I changed gears and left that out. I couldn't give them anything specific. What had I seen? A shadow. Houdini had me spooked. Maybe I'd imagined it. If I told them I'd seen a bear, they would've laughed or thrown me in the drunk tank. So, no, I didn't report it that way. Told them everything else exactly how it happened though.

BK: Why wasn't the body ever reported in the news? That's in the police report, but I never found that part of the story anywhere else.

G: Bad look for the community. The cops didn't want ordinary folks living in that area thinking there was a killer on the loose. You'd be surprised how many migrant deaths out here never make the news. It's like two worlds. No one cares. Not even in the migrant community. These folks come up here, braving who knows what with human smugglers and drug cartels to get across the border, and if they survive that far they kind of disappear into society. Second-class citizens. Living in the shadows. Trying to make their way and send money home, and they don't know anyone and no one knows them. They're alone. No roots. They go missing or die? Family back home only knows the money stops coming. Did their son, brother, or husband die? Did they just ditch them for a new life? Who knows? Not even other migrants know them well enough to care whether or not their deaths get a couple paragraphs from the *Chronicle*. They don't want to draw attention to themselves. The cops don't want to make a stink of crimes they know they'll never solve.

BK: Can't solve or won't solve?

G: You're a smart fellow. You already know the answer to that.

BK: This happens a lot?

G: Not a lot, no, but it happens. More than it should if you think it shouldn't ever happen, like me. No one really knows the numbers, though. How could they? We don't even know how many folks are living here in the cracks, and I guarantee not all of them who die are found.

BK: So it's conceivable a few migrant workers might die every year without anyone noticing?

G: Oh, yeah, 100 percent.

CHAPTER FIVE

After I pried loose and ripped away the first sheet of plywood, the rest came down fast, creating an entrance to the house. Annetta and I turned on our flashlights and stepped inside. Stale, moldy air coated our throats and set our eyes itching. Smashed furniture lay everywhere, just as Gary had described. A pile of personal belongings — a pair of old sneakers, a hoodie from the Riverhead Aquarium, two rolls of toilet paper, a comb, a toothbrush, and other odds and ends — lay in a moldering pile by the back window. The damage had knocked out some of the supporting structure, so the place's floors slanted, and its walls tilted at angles. The house creaked and groaned with our every step.

"Is this safe?" Annetta said. "Sounds like it's going to fall on our heads."

Playing my light along the wrecked front of the house exposed a sag where the ceiling dipped down into the absence left by a demolished support beam. Plywood had hidden the severity of it from the outside, but seeing it clearly, I shared Annetta's anxiety.

"I wouldn't say it's safe, no. Want to leave?" I said.

"Not after we came all this way. Let's be careful, though," she said. "It's stood this long; we can gamble on it holding together another hour."

"Agreed. But maybe we skip the second floor?" I said.

"All right, yeah, and let's be quick."

We rummaged through the place, shuffling disarrayed furniture and ordinary household objects scattered everywhere, seeking anything noteworthy. The living room divulged nothing of interest, so we moved to the kitchen then onto other first-floor rooms. A queen bed, neatly made and frosted with dust, occupied one bedroom. Beside it on a nightstand stood a lamp, a clock radio, a mug printed with a faded picture of local landmark the Big Duck, and a tattered copy of John Keel's *The Mothman Prophecies*, the edition with the Frank Frazetta cover. I riffled the pages. Handwritten notes filled the margins. I tucked it under my arm.

The second bedroom contained a dragon's hoard of books. Built-in shelves lined all four walls, with carve-outs for the windows. Orderly stacks of books covered two card tables. A reclining easy chair squatted in the room's center. Annetta and I split up to skim the books, every last one about some esoteric topic or another. If I'd imagined a complete library of cryptozoology, psychic phenomena, weird events, UFO encounters, strange history, cosmology, and pseudoscience, it would've looked like this room. A who's who of authors who'd made their careers separating fact from fiction or mixing the two: Jerome Clark, Loren Coleman, Stanton Friedman, R. T. Gould, Rosemary Ellen Guiley, J. Allen Hynek, John Keel, Donald Keyhoe, Nick Redfern, Jacques Vallée, Erich von Däniken, and others. So many others. Books shelved two deep. Books stacked on top of books. Tote bags piled with books not yet cataloged. The entire world of the weird compacted into a single room.

"I'm deeply impressed at this guy's commitment." Annetta pulled a couple of books from one of the shelves, then drew out two more from the second layer, wiped a skin of dust from the covers to read the titles then replaced them. "Assuming he'd read all these, not just hoarded them, he would've been a formidable expert."

"So why hasn't anyone ever heard of him?" I said. "He knew his stuff. He was doing original research. But he lived here like a hermit? It doesn't add up."

"Paranoia, maybe? He was afraid of someone stepping on his findings before he was ready to publish? Or no one would publish him? That would explain why he used a vanity press. He wasn't exactly a hermit. He taught botany. He had colleagues at Sagtikos U. They missed him. Some people keep their obsessions to themselves," Annetta said. "I dated a guy who seemed totally normal. Had a good family. Good job in finance. Dressed well. Played fantasy football with his pals every season. Then I discovered he was obsessed with the Acme Storyverse."

"So what? I love those old cartoons."

"Me too. But neither of us has a locked basement room filled with nothing but Connie Caribou memorabilia. He had *every*thing. Seriously. I could almost understand collecting the toys and books, but he had lunchboxes, girl pajamas and underwear, boxes of diapers, kids Halloween costumes, pillows and bedding, coloring books, everything. If Connie Caribou appeared on it, he owned it. All of it immaculate and unopened and perfectly organized."

"No judgment, but that's…"

"Oh, no, baby, judge away! That is full-on freaky in all the wrong ways. That's why he kept it all a secret. I only found out by accident. Maybe Mr. Burgess felt people just wouldn't understand and wanted to protect his reputation."

"This stuff isn't half as weird as a secret Connie Caribou stash."

"Not to you and me. Not now. Forty years ago? Geeks still occupied the lowest circle of social hell."

A fair point, but it left me unsatisfied. "Then why publish a book and put his name on it?"

"Best of both worlds. He sees his name on a book, but he doesn't have to worry about the public finding out."

"Okay, let's run with that. Burgess writes the book. Decides to publish it himself. Maybe he'll give copies away to trusted friends and colleagues. How did Stuffy Jones's uncle score one?"

"His uncle was a botanist, like Stuffy is, like Burgess was. Or *is* if he's still alive. Maybe they had a professional connection, and Burgess took a chance on letting him read it."

Another plausible explanation. Annetta excelled at finding them — or inventing them — and we needed them to keep us honest, but this one left me wishing for more.

I opened the room's one closet, probably for the first time in a decade. It stank of dust and aged paper. More books filled built-in shelves. A bankers box took up half a shelf at eye level, the only thing there other than books. I slid it out and popped the lid, exposing neat rows of binders and notebooks.

"What'd you find?"

Annetta slid out a notebook. Handwriting filled every page. Clean cursive from top to bottom, both sides, the entire volume. She took out a second and foukmnd the same. The binders held additional pages of handwritten notes tucked into clear plastic sleeves with maps, newspaper clippings, and other ephemera. On the cover of the first notebook Annetta examined were scrawled the words "Natura Occulta: Volume Two."

"He wrote another book," I said. "Or was in the process of writing it."

"Wild," Annetta said. "He never published it. What if he wrote it for himself, like a diary or a journal? Should we read it? Are we invading his privacy?"

"We're way past 'should' at this point. We started the investigation. We broke in here to find exactly this or something like it. We can't not read it. What if it leads us to the Peconic River Monster? What if it gives us a clue about what happened to the guy? We might solve his disappearance."

"Right, you're right. We absolutely read it," she said.

The house shuddered with a long crackling groan of shifting lumber, glass, and drywall. A loud thud reverberated up from below, quaking through the floor, our feet, into our muscles and bones. A vibration hummed through everything. Annetta grabbed onto me. She looked up, waiting for the ceiling to fall and streamers of dust to rain down around us. It held. When the disturbance faded, she let go.

"That came from the basement," I said.

"Please don't say you want to go look," said Annetta.

"Want to? Nope. We kind of have to, don't we? Or we might leave something important behind here. Do you want to take what we've got and go only to learn later we have to come back for something we missed?"

"No. I don't want to come back ever. Let's go check the damn cellar then hustle out of here."

I put the Keel book from Burgess's nightstand into the bankers box then deposited the container outside the hole where the front door once stood. Annetta and I retraced our steps until we located the basement entrance. The stairs looked and felt solid underfoot. The damage to the front and second floor of the house seemed to have left the basement unscathed. Instead of creaking and cracking, it absorbed sound. We descended into stony quiet and air so thick and humid it immediately wicked water along my arms. I tasted dampness. Whatever pollutants lingered in the air set my eyes on fire, itching.

From the bottom of the stairs, we cast around with our flashlights.

Dirt floor, whitewashed cement walls, an oil tank and a furnace, hot-water heater, washer and dryer, and nothing else. An ordinary functional basement. Light filtered in through windows spattered with dried mud from a recent rainstorm. Annetta found the steel fire door set into the cinderblock wall near the back of the space before I did. The hasp of a broken padlock dangled from an eye hook on the door. I flicked it loose, raised the plate, then opened it.

Air thick with moisture and an alien, animal musk clouded out.

I covered my mouth and coughed. Annetta gagged.

We recoiled from the door and waited until the foulness abated. As we entered, I flashed a light ahead of us to reveal a space larger than the rest of the basement. Half looked original to the foundation, but at some point, one wall had been removed, the earth excavated, and an area the size of a two-car garage added. At the room's center, a brick circle, three-feet high and ten feet in diameter, contained a pool of water. In the far corner lay mounds of old paper, drop cloths, leaves, dried grass, a stained mattress ripped open with batting spilling out, and other debris, forming a nest.

Nest.

The word came to mind without hesitation.

I circled the pool, knelt down next to the nest for a closer look. Sifting through the clutter, I recognized a piece of paper as part of Burgess's book. I shimmied it loose, tugging along most of the book with it.

Straightening up, I kicked a few things with my foot and ran my light over the mess. At the base of the structure lay a dozen cardboard boxes, split open, deteriorating with age, their contents — hundreds or thousands of copies of *Natura Occulta* — spilled all around them, tamped down, shredded, worked into the foundation of the massive nest. My joke about Reginald Burgess's basement filled with copies of his vanity-printed book struck me as bittersweet and uncomfortably accurate.

I raised my camera and snapped pictures, moving fast, trying to capture all sides of the room so we could get the hell out of there. The place rang every alarm bell in my head. I shot the nest from multiple angles, then the pool, capturing Annetta at its edge as she peered down into it. She angled her flashlight to the water. *Click.* Her eyes widened. *Click.* She gasped. *Click.* She recoiled from the well. I rushed to her side then looked into the water. Submerged deep in the well, at the limit of our light, a broad, monstrous face with glimmering tusks looked back. I saw it for a second at most, before it sank from sight. A trail of bubbles popped on the surface. Annetta and I looked at each other, terrified of admitting we hadn't imagined it. Then horror at our proximity to such a thing struck us, and we clutched each other's hands.

A ruckus sounded from outside, reaching us dimly, but ominously, in the basement.

The well gurgled. Outside water splashed on the riverbank. A fervent thudding filled the yard. The crack and splinter of vinyl drove a spike of fear through me. Annetta and I ran, taking the stairs two at a time, dashing through the house, the gaping hole that once held a front door. We hit the ground and raced around to the river side. In the water, a lithe, bulky shadow skimmed beneath the surface, trailing a soft wake, before it vanished from view with a trail of bubbles. On the bank, our kayaks and paddles lay smashed as if a giant fist had pounded them from the sky, crushed them to brightly colored splinters of aluminum and vinyl. The ground around them looked trampled, grass pressed flat, the soft edge of the bank peppered with enormous footprints. I shot pictures of the river, hoping for something to surface, but nothing did. I settled for photos of the demolished kayaks and the footprints in the mud. Footprints twice the size of my hand.

"What the hell was that?" I said.

"I've never seen anything like it," Annetta said. "It was too big to be… *anything* known to live around here."

"Does it live in the basement?"

"Something lives there."

"Whoa, is that what happened to Burgess? Did he try to hide it, then it… killed him?"

"I don't know, Ben. I don't know what to make of any of this." Annetta gripped my shoulder. "The box! The notes!"

She sprinted off, me on her heels, to the front of the house, where the bankers box sat right where we'd left it, untouched.

"Oh, thank god," Annetta said. "I was afraid that thing might've dragged it off."

I crouched on my haunches, lifted the box lid, and stared in at the undisturbed contents.

"Think the answer's in here?"

"I sure hope so," said Annetta. "We've got a more urgent question. How the hell do we get back to the kayak rental launch?"

In all the excitement, the problem hadn't even occurred to me. We'd left our car parked miles downriver where we began the day's journey. I pulled out my phone, opened an app, and scanned the screen. "Uber, I guess. Looks like we've got a car not too far from here. I'm pretty sure we're going to have to pay for those kayaks, though."

"What do we tell them happened?" Annetta said.

"The truth?"

"That a mystery monster smashed them? We found them that way after we finished breaking and entering? You want to piss them off, so they sue us or call the cops?"

"Right, right, okay, we say we beached them, but not high enough, went exploring, and when we got back, they were gone. Drifted away. We don't know where. Simple enough."

"Fine, call the Uber, then let's hide the wreckage. No point leaving it for someone to find and call us on our lie," Annetta said.

I summoned the Uber then returned to the wrecked kayaks.

I set my foot alongside one of the footprints. The size difference made me feel exactly like that hamster let loose from its safe little home into the big wild world. Prey discovering for the first time the existence of predators. By the time we finished dragging the kayak wreckage into tall grass and covering it with fallen leaves and branches, a black car sat at the curb. Neither I nor Annetta had heard it arrive. A four-door sedan, a third longer than any contemporary car, sloped toward the trunk like a panther ready to pounce, finished off with tail fins that resembled harpoons. Tinted windows all around, even the front windshield, reflected the ruined house and surrounding trees, a window into another world. The black finish glistened in the daylight. The mild afternoon turned chilly. A thick cloud crossed the sun, spilling shadows on the overgrown lawn and chapped asphalt. The driver's side window rolled down.

"That's not our Uber, is it?" Annetta said.

I offered no answer. The subtly old-fashioned lines of the car, the absence of any model or make indicators or a manufacturer's logo, and the soft whir and whistle of its idling engine sufficed.

"It's been so long, I thought maybe they'd forgotten about us."

I called out to the car: "What do you want?"

From the open window emerged a pale hand, flat and spongy, with fingers like the branches of a birch tree, extruding from a white shirt cuff and a black jacket sleeve. The fingers gestured for us to approach.

"We're good right here," I said.

The hand withdrew into the vehicle.

"We could run through the woods to one of the neighboring streets," Annetta said.

"They'd follow us. Catch up with us somewhere else," I said.

"Then why don't we go over there and be done with it?"

"I don't want to make it easy for them."

The more we drew out the Men in Black, the more they might reveal of themselves. I still didn't fully understand their nature or the role they'd played in our encounter with the Montauk Monster. They kept their distance, so any insight could help. The hand reappeared and gestured more fervently. A dully resonant voice said, "Come closer, please."

"No," I said. "You come here."

The hand snapped back, out of sight.

"Do we want to piss them off?" said Annetta. "We have no idea what they might do."

I met her eyes, filled with caution but not fear. We'd lived with the park rangers keeping tabs on our comings and goings so long that fear had become tedious. We weren't used to them, no, but we'd grown accustomed to their presence. Despite the long break since we'd last seen them, their return didn't surprise me. I'd anticipated it when we began our investigation of the Peconic River Monster.

The driver's and passenger's doors opened simultaneously. A man emerged from either side of the car, each one thin, better than six-feet tall, and wearing a long black overcoat atop a black suit, tie, and white shirt, with a black fedora pitched low on their brows. The passenger drew several items out of the trunk and handed some to the driver. In moments, they set up a small folding table and four folding lawn chairs, all solid black. The driver gestured at the seats.

"Let's meet halfway," he said.

Their hat brims shaded their faces except for the flat, waxy lines of their lips above chins like melted spatulas. Annetta and I nodded agreement to each other before we crossed the weedy lawn and accepted two seats.

"What do you want?" I said.

"Lovely day, isn't it?" the driver said.

"Why are you following us?"

"How do you like this neighborhood? Is it a good place to raise a family?" the passenger said.

"I don't know. I don't live here. Why are you here?" I said.

"Why do you follow us?" said Annetta.

"A man lived here once, but he had no family," the driver said.

"That's the story," I said.

"Then I suppose he couldn't answer our question, either," said the driver.

"He lived here with no family, but not alone," said the passenger.

"Not alone, no," the driver said.

"Do you need a ride?" said the passenger.

"What the hell do you want from us?" I said.

"We heard you had an accident. Your boat sank," the passenger said.

"Yeah, right, our boat sank," said Annetta.

"That's right," I added. "Can you get us a new one?"

"Do you need a ride?" the driver said.

"I don't think we can fit you both. Our car is too small," said the passenger.

"Much too small," the driver said. "We're not going your direction anyway."

"How do you know which direction we're going?" Annetta said.

The Men in Black exchanged a glance with invisible eyes.

"Well, we're not going that direction," the driver said. "We have a schedule. Have you lived in this house long?"

"No," I said. "We've never lived here."

"Such a nice house," the passenger said.

"Do you know about the basement? About the thing that lives there?" I said.

"I know all about the basement," the driver said. "In this neck of the woods, most houses have basements. Sometimes cellars. All sorts of creatures live in them. Crickets. Millipedes. Spiders. Termites."

"We're sorry your boat sank. Perhaps it's best. Some journeys aren't meant to be completed," said the passenger. "Destinations aren't necessary when the journey is its own reward."

"You won't tell anyone what you saw on your journey," the driver said.

A statement, not a question. An order, not a request.

"They won't tell a soul. They know better," the passenger said. "Secrets shared are no longer secrets. Journeys end in lovers meeting. These lovers have met. Journey's end."

"So you understand? We can't give you a ride no matter how deep your boats sank," said the driver. He stood, folded his chair, then tucked it under his arm. He gazed up at the ruined house. The sun penetrated the deep shade of his hat brim, illuminating the hollows of his deep-sunk sockets. "A shame how the place has gone downhill."

The passenger stood, folded his chair, then handed it to the driver, who gathered it together with his own chair. Next, he folded the table and passed that off too. The driver carried them to the car. The trunk opened, seemingly on its own. The passenger gestured at the seats Annetta and I occupied.

"We hope you enjoyed our chairs."

Unsure of what else to do, we stood. The passenger folded our chairs then handed them off to the driver who carried them to the trunk. His overcoat flapping in the breeze, he crossed the lawn to where Reginald Burgess's bankers box waited by the curb.

"This too?" he said.

Only a force I can't explain, a primal instinct to hold back more powerful than the instinct to bolt to the box and snatch it up kept me from interfering.

The driver straightened from stowing the chairs. "I... think not. At least, not today." A wave of relief rushed through me, as he swiveled, his overcoat rippling, to face me and Annetta. "You know how to dispose of that waste? It's not doing anyone any good."

"Man, I don't know what to do with any of this. You need to make some sense," I said.

His lips animated for the first time, hinted at an off-putting smile. "Excellent! We agree."

"There are some pages missing," the passenger said. "Don't worry. Nothing important."

The trunk closed by itself as the driver opened the car door and slid into the driver's seat. The passenger slipped in on the other side. The driver's side window rolled up. The car purred and scraped away from the curb, circled, then exited from sight. Immediately, my cell phone rang, startling me out of whatever weird haze had overtaken me. Annetta jumped too. I answered our frustrated Uber driver, who'd roamed River Road four times without any luck finding our pick-up spot. I looked at his location on the map. No more than fifty yards from Estuary Dr.

"Try again. You're right on top of us. Take the next right," I told him.

With the park rangers and their black car gone, he found the turn right away.

Minutes later Annetta and I watched the road as the driver steered away from the broken-down house at 4 Estuary Drive, the bankers box stowed between us for the drive back to the kayak rental office where we'd parked our car.

Chapter Six

The rental office charged us full price for the two kayaks and missing paddles plus a fifteen percent replacement fee. The owner, Mr. Owens, interrogated us but gave up with a sneer when we stuck to our story. I doubt he believed us about the kayaks drifting off, but he didn't question it further once we paid. We drove home with the bankers box on the backseat.

Home these days consisted of a house that belonged to the mother of one of Annetta's work friends. She only occupied the little cottage near the Long Island Sound during the warm weather, living the rest of the year in her Florida condo. A recent hip fracture left her stuck in the Sunshine State indefinitely. We were doing them a favor by house-sitting. At the same time, no one else knew where we were living, while my house in Hicksville sat empty, checked on now and then by a neighbor who'd been close with my parents. The Men in Black could find us anywhere, but the cottage hid us from anyone using ordinary means to track us down.

At home, we organized what we'd gathered from the house on Estuary Drive on the dining room table. A dozen notebooks and reams of paper printed with Burgess's book, the second of three intended volumes mapping his personal history with nature's secrets, dating back to his childhood in Australia. The pages and notebooks were out of order. Annetta and I collated major portions of it into stacks of related writings. We wouldn't know, though, if we'd gotten it right until we sat down and read the thing through. Even then we'd still be guessing.

What had Reg Burgess done? Where had he gone? Why did any of it matter?

No one else on earth seemed to miss the guy or spend any more time looking for him than the obligatory police investigation, long-ago shoved into the cold case file. My buzzing phone upended my thoughts as I sifted through pages. I ignored it, engrossed in some of Reg's work, until Annetta nudged me under the table, looking at the screen over papers in her hand.

"It's Malik," she said.

I swiped the screen and held the phone to my ear. "Hey, Malik, how's it going? What can I do for you?"

"What can you do for me? You can buy my house so I can move the hell out of here," he said. The anxiety in his voice worried me. A retired New York sheriff, Malik Campbell did not scare easily or back down from trouble, as Annetta and I had learned when he helped us investigate the Montauk Monster, but he sounded near his limit. "They're back, man. They're back."

"Who's back?" I said.

"The damn Bigfoots. Man, remember how I figured it would be easy to catch one of the things, parade it around, and prove its existence to everyone? What a laugh, right? It's like trying to grab a bag of water with these things. They're here then they're gone, and when they're here, they're in your life like rats. You think they're gone because you don't see them for months, years, then they turn up again. So what you can do for me is leave me the hell out of anything to do with any of this."

"With what?"

"With goddamn Bigfoot, the weirdos in the black cars, and all the rest of it."

"You've seen them?"

"Every night for the last week. Half an hour ago before I called you when my cell signal finally came back. I seen 'em, heard 'em, *smelled* 'em. The missus already skipped out to her sister's. This time I'm going with her. I can't take another go round with this stuff. It's like… they want *us* to see 'em and know about 'em but no one else. You know? They're playing games, and I don't feel like jumping through their hoops anymore."

"What have you seen this time?"

"Not too much of the Bigfoots. They've been keeping clear of the house. I hear them knocking trees out in the Pine Barrens. All night long some nights. Haven't slept worth a damn in weeks. Every day, right around dusk, their stink drifts out of the woods. I have to keep the windows shut tight. Those goons in the black cars cruise by my house.

I catch them in the rearview mirror when I'm driving through town. What do they want, Ben? Are they checking up on me? I gave up on all this. What are they after?"

"No idea."

I told Malik about our investigation of the Peconic River creature, our encounter with the Men in Black that afternoon.

"Dammit! You stirred it all up again," he said, then he gave a long sigh. "All right, listen. I'm out of here in the morning. You want to try and communicate with them, get some answers, my place is yours. You know where to find the spare key. I'm hooking up with Janae tomorrow for a vacation down south. I hope all this is done and over when we get back. Give Annetta my best. And, Ben? Be safe."

The call disconnected. I dropped my phone on the table and summed it up for Annetta.

"You think it's like with the Montauk Monster?" she said. "They want us to stop something trying to break through to our world?"

"I think something's already here. We need to figure out what it is and why this is kicking up now. I doubt it was a coincidence that Stuffy Jones's uncle died and sent Burgess's book your way." I tapped a stack of manuscript pages. "Fingers crossed we find some answers here."

We dug into Burgess's manuscript, but neither of us made it far before the day caught up with us and exhaustion sent us to bed. Later, in the smallest hours, I awoke sweating, eyes open, paralyzed for a moment, and gasped for breath. Downstairs, the floor creaked. A piece of furniture thumped. A muffled voice swore. Annetta lay beside me, sleeping, her breath rising, falling with a reassuring pulse. I snapped on the bedside light.

More low voices. Footsteps.

I woke Annetta, making sure she saw me gesture to stay quiet when she opened her eyes. I indicated downstairs, pointed to my ear. *Listen.* The voices spoke again, unintelligible, but she heard them. She snatched up her cell phone. I slid my hand across the screen and shook my head. In the nightstand drawer I kept a .38 revolver. I removed it and eased myself off the bed. Annetta threw me a look. *Don't be stupid.* I shook my head again then slipped from the bedroom. The cottage's second floor contained only the master bedroom, a bathroom, and the landing atop the stairs, which descended to the living room. Lying down and craning my neck along the first step, I peered into the dining room where lights and shadows moved.

I wanted to crawl back to Annetta, call 911, and wait out the invasion. But 911 would make our presence here official. We'd have to move on to keep our low profile. Lights and sirens would scare away the intruders. I wanted to know who they were. I crouched on the landing then crab-walked down the stairs, my eye on the dining room door, revolver pointed the same direction. At the bottom of the steps, I straightened and braced myself. My heart beat like a small child trapped inside me trying to punch his way out of my chest. Adrenalin rushes washed through me. I tightened my grip on the .38, then lunged into the dining room.

"Who's here?" I shouted.

The lights vanished. Dancing shadows dissolved to solid gloom.

My eyes lagged behind the motion, leaving me in a blind panic as I slapped the wall with my left hand until it found the switch and filled the room with shocking brightness. I looked between the china cabinet and the hutch, even under the table. Nothing. No one. One of two windows gaped open. A weak breeze set the end of the curtain twitching. I dashed across the room and looked outside through the screen.

Darkness. Lights down the road, too far to illuminate the little yard.

The lacy tangle of the delicate rose bushes in front of the window, undisturbed.

Ordinary night sounds.

Annetta arrived behind me.

"Who was here?" she said. "Where did they go?"

I didn't know how to explain the instantaneous departure of our intruders, but I tried my best. Annetta didn't understand it, but she didn't question me.

"Did they take anything?" she said.

Everything in the dining room looked undisturbed down to the thin layer of dust that coated the china cabinet. The papers on the table looked untouched, but, no, something felt out of order. I scanned the stacks, one to the next to the next, counting them, weighing the height of each against my memory, trying to recall if this or that page had been out of place when we'd gone to bed — then it clicked.

"They didn't take anything," I said. "They left us something."

"What are you talking about?"

"Look in the box."

The bankers box sat open on the table. We had emptied it completely while sorting out the manuscript pages. Inside of it now sat a large manila envelope stuffed to the breaking point.

CHAPTER SEVEN

From the papers of Reginald Burgess, a possible chapter of Natura Occulta, *Volume Two, unpublished. Reprinted from a notebook marked "The Secret Code of Billabongs and Waterways."*

Where? Western Australia.

More specific? East or south of Sydney. Fifty, a hundred, three hundred kilometers.

Way out beyond the black stump.

Remote. Lonely. Water. A river. A lake or a billabong. A secret place.

My father took me camping there. A place no one else knew. A family place, he told me, known to his father, his grandfather, and his great-grandfather, passed down to me with a responsibility beyond my naiveté to understand the first time we went there. I savvied enough, though, to know recording its precise location for strangers to go tromping about would compromise it. So I did as my father asked and tried not to think about that place or its geographic features when we weren't there. *You ought to have blindfolded me for the trip,* I joked. The way he hesitated before laughing told me he'd considered it.

After hours of driving, we arrived in the heat of the day and made camp, immediately seeking shelter in the shade of our tent. My father's Land Rover sat fifty meters away, the closest it could travel to the campsite: a clearing above water that glittered like a blue-sequined dress. It called to my young heart. I imagined kicking off my trainers, stripping away my sweaty clothes then leaping from the high ledge to plunge into pure, liquid coolness. My father, guessing my mind from how my gaze lingered on the water, shook his head.

"No swimming. Not here, not ever, Reg," he said.

My hopes for relief casually dashed, I frowned. "Why not?"

"Water here isn't safe."

Snakes and spiders. Sharks. Carnivorous fish. Whirlpools. Rip currents. So many possibilities flooded my imagination without regard for plausibility. The water took on a new dimension. A strong swimmer, I'd always considered water a source of sustenance and joy. Now its beautiful ripples and countless glints of reflected sun hid danger. Even more compelling to my young mind, it hid a mystery because my father refused to elaborate on his warning. *Don't go in the water. Don't ask me why. End of discussion.* His reticence fueled my curiosity. I peppered him with questions, guesses, and speculations, all left unanswered. He reclined on his sleeping bag, yanked his hat over his face, and told me to have a nanna's.

"Too hot for much this time of day anyway. We've a long night ahead of us," he said.

Moments later, his snores filled the tent.

The water downhill, visible through the mesh across the open tent flap, entranced me. My brain raced with the tantalizing dilemma. What did the water hide? What made it dangerous enough for my father, who often swam with me in the ocean, to keep us out? Twelve years old, I inhabited that childhood twilight of infinite possibilities when the world still holds true magic, a sensibility we lose not all at once, but by degrees, closing one door after another onto the things we hope or believe, as a child, might be real. Santa Claus, the Tooth Fairy, and the Easter Bunny. The Boogeyman. Magic wands and cloaks. Flying carpets. Three wishes from a genie's lamp. Dinosaurs and prehistoric sharks surviving into the present. Aliens visiting our planet. We find it easy to close those doors as our understanding of the world deepens. The unlikelihood of those things crushes us with logic. The next set to close comes harder. The hope we might grow up to become a star athlete, a brilliant musician, a world leader, or the genius doctor who cures cancer. For a precious few, those doors stay open, but the rest of us can only jam them ajar as long as we resist reality. At age twelve, all my doors remained open.

My father, a surveyor, knew well the Outback, which he'd measured and catalogued in long stints away from home, before my mother took ill, and he traded his bush trips for a desk job.

This jaunt marked his first excursion back since mum passed away, our first ever together. We both needed the change of scenery, a fact I recognize more in retrospect than I did then. We needed a catalyst to reset the dynamic of our relationship as a family of two, a painful, unavoidable adjustment.

Happy for time with my dad away from constant reminders of my mother's last agonizing months, I tried my to do what he asked. I closed my eyes, certain I'd never nap while all the questions bounced around inside me, but nap I did, only awakening to my father's gentle prodding and darkness outside our tent. I sat up, surprised, and rubbed slumber from my eyes.

Insects chirped and buzzed, filling the air with electric music. The water resembled a photo negative of the afternoon, black as tar, softly chapped by moonlight. My dad motioned me out of the tent then led me along a narrow, rocky trail that rose over the water. At its peak, we laid down, side by side, behind a stand of overgrown spinifex then wormed forward until we obtained a perfect view of the water. I lost count of how often I asked what we were doing, where we were going, what we would see. One after another, Dad deflected my questions, until I gave up and waited in silence. Waited a long time, worried I might doze off again and miss the big event. The moon traversed half the night sky before my father gripped my arm and warned me—no matter what— not to move from our hiding spot.

"You're a good lad, there, Reg. I know you've got it in you. The age is important," he said. "Too young, and you believe, but you've got no sense of the gravity of it. Too old, you'll rationalize it away because your brain's just go no space left for it." He talked to himself more than me, as if easing his own qualms. "Twelve-years-old, that's the perfect age. My age when your grandfather brought me to this very place to see what you'll see tonight."

I'd never met my grandfather. My image of him grew from seeds my father planted when he spoke about him, cultivating him into a figure larger than life. A genius builder and a bushman without peer. How might I have felt about that night if I'd ever met the man himself?

Long moments stretched into longer seconds, accumulated into interminable minutes, and I feared Dad had gotten it wrong. Brought us to the wrong place. Or on the wrong night. Then, a few meters off, the water frothed. Bubbles spawned, translucent ivory billiard balls in the moon glow. They travelled toward us. A shape rose beneath the water, not quite breaking the surface. A moving mass that shimmied, wriggled, and swam a meandering course toward our hidden spot. It filled me with wonder and fright. What could it be? All my guesses popped into my mind. None matched what I saw. None even came close. A whale, I thought, knowing no whale could live in this water. A hippopotamus. A plesiosaur. None of it made sense. Nor did the shape that emerged provide any ready answers.

Water flowed off it as it climbed onto a small beach on the opposite bank. A thick-legged beast with a sinuous body covered in the oddest mix of hair, scales, and feathers. Its pendulous head weighed heavy on a stringy neck thrusting from between its knobby shoulders. It stretched, twisted, and opened a massive mouth gated by tusks the length of sabers rising from its lower jaw. Moonlight set its eyes rippling with colour. Its mouth stretched wider, a crater funnelling to a wide throat, then it snapped its jaws shut and released a huff of breath that rattled in my ears. My father steadied me, a hand on my shoulder. His gaze locked on the creature. The biggest smile I'd ever seen on him creased his lips.

"A beauty," he whispered to me. "A real beauty. Don't you think, Reg?"

Awed and confused, I struggled to answer.

"No telling how much longer she'll be with us. That's our job, Reggie. Our pact."

"What do you mean, Pop?"

I received no answer that night.

My father's demeanor soured in a snap. His smile evaporated. Wonder fled from his eyes as the creature lifted itself on its haunches. Its head tilted, nose sniffing as it tried to suss out the location of whatever it smelled.

"Oh, no, no, not tonight, please, not now," my dad said.

He ordered me to stay put, no matter what, then pushed himself onto his hands and knees before he hurried back along the trail to our camp. Across the way, the creature shifted then slid back into the water without the slightest splash and swam in the same direction. The next moment, lights appeared across the water. Voices followed. High-pitched laughter. Playful squeals. A teenage boy and a girl roamed into view. Even my young mind knew they were sneaking away from a party or a camp for some romantic privacy. They descended the opposite bluff to the little beach, pulling off their clothes as they went. They meant to go swimming — in water my father called dangerous. What to do? Stay put and quiet as I'd promised my dad? Jump up and shout a warning at them but give myself away? My dad spared me the decision.

Light winked on to my left. The two lovers stiffened in surprise as my dad cried out across the water then caught them in their state of undress with a powerful, battery-powered spotlight. He yelled for them to stay out of the water, get off the beach, they shouldn't be here on this night, that they were in danger and needed to listen to him immediately. All the things one might say to people too angry and stubborn to hear words meant to save their lives. The girl shouted nasty insults at my dad, calling him a pervert and a peeping tom, while she recovered her clothes and dressed. The man didn't bother with clothes. He stood in his boxer shorts on the beach, shaking his fist, hollering at my father to shut off the light, get on out of here, challenging him to a fight when my dad refused. Furious and ignoring my dad's frantic warnings to stay clear of the water, the man stamped into the shallows up to his knees, screaming curses, saliva spraying from his lips in the high-powered light.

The creature struck so fast I doubted my eyes.

The water surged. The thing emerged, mouth wide, tusks spread apart like the prongs of a massive staple remover. They snapped shut around the man's waist. As swiftly as it had pounced, it dragged him under the water, leaving him no chance to even scream, as it retreated from the beach.

For a heartbeat, the thing had hung poised in the blazing light of my father's high-powered torch. What had seemed mysterious, noble, and wonderful by gentle moonlight, ignited the first real terror I had ever felt. I screamed. The woman screamed. The man simply vanished. Hysterical, the woman scrambled up the bluff into the darkness. I couldn't look away from the water. I waited for the man or creature to resurface and show me I hadn't just watched someone die. Neither ever did. The water regained its nocturnal calm. My father scooped me up and returned us to camp. He placed me in the Land Rover then struck our tent, packed our gear, and drove us away.

I said nothing the whole ride home, shocked, incapable of understanding what I'd seen or why my father had shown it to me. I vaguely understood he hadn't intended for me to see the awful attack. The teenagers had come along at the wrong time. That didn't reassure me. Nor did my father's worries about the black car that followed us down the highway back to Sydney.

I'd already been introduced to one shocking danger that night at our campsite. My child's mind struggled to make sense of that. It would be a long time before I understood the danger of the black cars.

Chapter Eight

Annetta paper-clipped several pages inside a notebook as she finished reading it. "This part reads right to me." She placed the notebook near stacks of pages and other notebooks we took as the early chapters of Reginald Burgess's unpublished manuscript, slowly compiled from the disorganized material. Burgess seemed to have grabbed notebooks and scrap paper at random to continue writing with no regard for picking up where he left off, looking only for the nearest blank page, making his story a jigsaw puzzle of jumbled pieces.

We'd spent the whole morning trying to make sense, not only of Burgess's writing, but of the previous night's break-in. After turning on every light inside and outside of the house, we'd sat up until dawn then walked the yard, finding no sign anyone had been there. No footprints and no handprints on the window that had been opened, one Annetta knew for sure she'd locked before we went to bed.

The envelope left in the box only sowed deeper confusion.

It contained more pages of Burgess's manuscript.

Missing or alternate pages? Neither Annetta nor I could even guess.

It seemed the invaders had substituted pages in the stacks we'd recovered from the house at 4 Estuary Drive with different versions then put the originals into the envelope. The pages in the envelope amounted to nothing coherent when read together in any order we tried. They contained fragments of a larger story missing too much context. The pages in the envelopes matched the paper from the banker's box, but we now found pages of a different paper stock, coarser and yellower than the rest, intermingled with the pages we'd already organized, even stuck into notebooks. At least, it seemed so. Given how tired we were the night before and how little time we'd spent familiarizing ourselves with the papers, we might've missed some details.

Whatever the intruders' purpose, nothing explained their instantaneous departure. One second, at least two people, from the sound of it, had fumbled around in our dining room. The next second, they were gone. The clocks eliminated any possibility that I'd lost time or blacked out. I'd glanced at one the moment before entering the dining room. It advanced only seconds by the time I turned on the dining room lights. Annetta feared the Men in Black had returned, but they interacted with us directly albeit in their weird way. This felt like someone trying to act subtly, clandestinely, even though they failed.

Annetta handed me another batch of pages she'd assembled. I read it through.

The order seemed correct. I jotted page numbers at the bottom, right corner of each sheet, then added it to the stack of likely complete chapters. Eventually, we'd have to figure out the sequence for the chapters and hope we had spare no pages. Burgess had left behind enough material for several books.

His writings ranged over every kind of cryptid and unusual phenomena. Before leaving Australia, he'd leveraged his botanical work and off-time from teaching to research everything from anomalous big cat sightings in the Otway Ranges to Oz's own version of Bigfoot, the Yowie. He'd stalked the Hawkesbury River Monster, an Australian Nessie; the Burrunjor, a reptilian El Chupacabra; and even the Yara-ma-yha-who, an ancient thing out of Aboriginal folklore. A dwarfish, red man with a swollen head and a toothless mouth, Yara-ma-yha-who jumped onto its victims from trees to feed its appetite for human meat through lamprey-like suckers on its fingertips. That one strained even Reg's seemingly limitless credulity. He dismissed this Outback vampire as a true cryptid and relegated it to pure myth.

Reg seemed to believe in every other wild possibility and outlandish claim, so his level-headed take on that case reassured me. Still, how much of his stories had he fabricated or written as hopeful thought-experiments? How much was real? How much crackpot? How many times did he pause on the path to look back and rethink those stepping stones behind him and re-envision the trail ahead? How often would Annetta and I do the same before we found the answers we sought?

We organized papers until late afternoon. Before dusk arrived, we packed everything back in the bankers box, gathered clothes for a few days, piled everything into the car, then—no longer feeling safe in the cottage after the break-in—we drove to Malik's house on Red Creek

Road at the edge of the Pine Barrens. The backdoor key waited right where expected, hidden under a stone near the unique shark-cage garden gazebo that memorialized our attempt to capture a Bigfoot.

Malik's car sat in the driveway, but he didn't make an appearance. Janae must have picked him up for their vacation. Inside, emptiness and stillness. The kitchen walls still showed fresh repairs where a Bigfoot had thrown a tree trunk through the window above the kitchen sink. Another house besieged by the unknown. It reminded me of 4 Estuary Drive, except Malik, Annetta, and I hadn't gone missing.

We spread Reg's papers in Malik's living room, on his coffee table, on the floor, on the sofa, everywhere we could find space. We ate frozen pizza then settled back into collating and compiling, but the darker it grew, the more Malik's phone call weighed on us. Would we hear the tree-crashing knocks the Bigfoots liked to make? Would we smell them? Would black cars park along the road? By midnight, we doubted it. We worked straight through, with breaks when I stepped outside to listen and take in the night air. I walked to the end of Malik's driveway and surveyed the street for black cars, but no cars at all sat parked anywhere. Hardly any drove by the house. Other than making progress with *Natura Occulta: Volume Two*, it seemed like a bust. No one knocked at the door. No one broke in. Nothing raised a ruckus in the neighboring Pine Barrens. Around 2 a.m., I persuaded Annetta to take the king-sized bed in Malik and Janae's room, while I sat up until sleep overcame me on the sofa, wanting to stay close if our weird intruders visited us here.

They didn't. Or if they did, I dozed through it. Either way, a restless night on the sofa ended at dawn, when Annetta woke me up and sent me into the bedroom to sleep while she took morning watch.

Three hours later, the aroma of coffee roused me from bed.

"You think maybe Malik was making stuff up? Or imagining it?" Annetta fixed us eggs and bacon from Malik's fridge while I drank coffee and struggled to shake off sleepiness. "Or Janae went all Scooby Doo villain to scare him into taking her on vacation?"

Annetta slid full plates onto the kitchen table, and we ate.

I laughed. "Hmmm, yeah, Janae always did give me an 'Old Man Withers' vibe." I gulped some coffee, burning my mouth in the process. "But no, I don't think any of those things. Malik knows what's what. If he said it happened, then it all happened like he said."

"Assuming that was Malik on the phone," she said.

That stopped me dead, a forkful of eggs halfway to my mouth. I set it back on my plate and took a deep breath. The Men in Black sometimes communicated via phone calls from nowhere, nonsensical numbers filling our cell phone screens. Sometimes their voices changed mid-sentence on a call. Could they have imitated Malik and sent us here on purpose?

"That hadn't occurred to me," I said.

"Me, either, until I saw this." Annetta rose and retrieved a calendar hanging from the wall beside the refrigerator. She placed it on the table and pointed to a notation in the box for a date almost a week past. It read "Vacay! Yay!" with a line extending for two weeks. "Malik called us less than 48 hours ago."

"This doesn't make sense."

"Nope."

"That was Malik's voice on the phone, no question. The stuff he reported isn't happening now because he's not here, and we are. It was meant only for him. That's all. That's how this works. One day, someone sees an impossible thing. Bigfoot in the woods. Aliens on a lonely highway. A prehistoric sea monster in the local lake. The next day, and the next day, and the next day after that—no one else ever sees it."

"Custom weirdness?"

"Right."

"Except Malik's car is here, and this calendar suggests his vacation wasn't spontaneous. Did he call from wherever he is with Janae? Did the stuff happen before they left, but he waited to tell us?"

"No. It was immediate, fresh. There was fear in his voice. The occurrences were driving him away from here."

"Does that sound like Malik, letting anything scare him away from his own home?"

"It doesn't. Shit. Who did I talk to on the phone?"

"What if Janae finally convinced him to take a real vacation? Then our black-suited pals noticed the house was empty and took advantage to get us out here? I've felt like a piece on someone's chessboard for a long time."

"Me, too." I ate and thought, then said, "Is any of this adding up?" Sliding my nearly empty plate aside, I sipped more coffee, then took up the nearest stack of papers. "The longer we work on Burgess's papers, the more it feels like it is, but is it painting a false picture? Are we imposing our own order to make sense of it, but it all means something else? How do we know what's right, what's real, what's accurate?"

"We don't." Annetta placed her hand on the back of mine. "Not yet. But we will."

"If the Men in Black mimicked Malik on the phone, why did they want us here?"

Annetta shrugged then laughed "Babe, your guess is as good as mine. The only thing I know for sure is that now — it's on. We're not letting go of this until we get some answers. We will understand this sooner or later because I'm beyond through with being anyone's pawn."

I smiled at her, grateful for her confidence, for supporting me through a moment of doubt, for her open mind, and her commitment to investigating whatever incredible situation we'd blundered into, even when it meant house-jumping, break-ins, and disruptions. My phone buzzed. I didn't recognize the number onscreen until a name appeared: Riverhead Canoe and Kayak Rentals. I answered, expecting the owner, Mr. Owens, with additional charges for the lost kayaks. Instead, the caller introduced himself as Officer Lou Nowak with the Riverhead Police. A fisherman in a canoe had spotted and reported our ruined kayaks, fearing someone might have been injured or drowned. Officer Nowak and the rental shop owner wanted an explanation for why we'd lied, wanted us to answer some questions, and could we come down to the shop to corroborate Mr. Owens's version of events. Annetta had to drive to Brooklyn that afternoon to teach, but I agreed to do my best to settle the issue.

"Why the hell do the cops care about a couple of busted-up kayaks we already paid for?" she said after I ended the call. "So we lied? We still paid to replace them and then some. Who cares why?"

"I guess because the owner sent his nephew, a high school kid who works for him part time, to gather the debris in one of the shop trucks," I said. "The kid found something else with the wreckage."

"Like what?"

"A corpse — part of one, at least."

Chapter Nine

From the papers of Reginald Burgess, possible chapter of Natura Occulta, Volume Two, *unpublished. Reprinted here from a notebook marked "Footprints in the Earth: Tracking the Yowie."*

The first time I really grasped the threat of the men who drove the black cars came two years after the night my father introduced me to the water monster. We'd gone straight home that night, no stops even for petrol, which left us praying to reach our carport for the last ten kilometers of our drive as the needle edged to empty. My father offered no explanations for what he'd shown me, only apologies that it hadn't gone as intended. He had meant for us to stay the night then hike along the trail in the morning to another secret spot. We'd fled to avoid contact with any authorities who might show up once the girl reported her boyfriend missing. Even at twelve, it frightened me that anything we'd done might require dodging the police. My father tried to warn them, after all. Then I thought of the names the boy and the girl called him and figured the police wouldn't like that part of what had happened.

In the following days, Dad brought home extra newspapers beyond our daily delivery of the *Sydney Morning Herald* and read every page, seeking, I suppose, some report of the beast or the man's disappearance. He never found one, as far as I know. In two weeks, he gave up, noticeably relieved.

A new routine settled upon us, awkward and uncomfortable at first without my mother or the need to care for her. I attended school. My father worked in his locked office at the back of the house or went to the local office of his employer. Sometimes he worked in the field, running survey projects in the city. He never traveled far, never into the bush. He never said anything more about that night, either. He told me only that I knew all I needed to know for now. He'd show me more at the right time. I pressed him, but he remained resolutely tight-lipped. Some nights I awoke late after going to bed to his voice talking in his bedroom, speaking as if my mother were still with him. It broke my heart and frightened me so much I stopped asking about anything out of the ordinary, worried I might push him over some incomprehensible edge my young mind couldn't define.

Two years passed. The memories of that night remained fresh, but I started to relinquish them as unfinished business we'd never resolve. Those open doors that surround us in youth closed one-by-one with each passing month. They slam shut fast in the teenage years, when the rush to adulthood speeds us toward maturity and the desire for others to perceive us as mature. Shun that kid stuff or risk life as a laughingstock, a fate worse than death in the teen world. I came around to thinking of what I'd seen that night as a hallucination. My young brain witnessed a terrible, but ordinary thing, a man drowning, and imprinted a monster onto it. My father warned the couple about water conditions, not an imaginary beast. The boy ignored him, sank underwater, and my horrified mind built a story to shield me. Or perhaps it had been a hoax, a game of some kind that went fatally wrong. The more I matured, the more my brain spackled over the implausible gaps with mundane explanations.

Until the day a black car followed me home from school.

The car must have tracked me for several days before I spotted it. I felt sure I'd glimpsed it out of the corner of my eye or amidst the other cars on the road, and, distracted by all the things that occupy a teenage boy's mind, overlooked its distinctiveness. It resembled the cars people drove in old movies but redesigned to blend with contemporary makes and models. Modest tail fins. Sleek rather than the boxy lines common at the time. It drove in near silence. The motor made little more than a low-cycle hum. Tinted windows concealed the occupants. The first time I looked right at it, it struck me as familiar, as if I'd seen it around school, or my neighborhood, or my town when my father and I went shopping. Present but never registered, not until it prowled ten meters behind me on an empty street with no other pedestrians to keep me company.

Only me and a weird black car.

What drew my attention to it? To this day, I'm unsure.

A very faint car horn tooting from another block? Or could it have been the car's own oddly muted horn? A voice calling my name? The electric *brrrr* of a power window lowering?

Whatever sparked my attention, I glanced over my shoulder to see it, a sight that startled me. I froze in place. The car stopped too. I took several steps. It followed, maintaining distance between us. I sped up to a jog. It kept perfect pace, the gap never changing. Afraid I'd become a target of kidnappers, I broke into a full run, dashed up a driveway, raced through one backyard, then the next one abutting it, then across the next street to do the same through two more yards, emerging onto a road two blocks over, and, to my dismay, farther from home. My heart sank even more when the car rounded the corner and caught up to me.

I shouted for help, but my voice carried no resonance, as if an air effect dampened it. No one came to my aid. No windows or front doors opened. No one ran from their yard to suss out the ruckus. I stood my ground. What else could I do? The car rolled up at the kerb and stopped. The driver's window lowered. Out of the blackness inside poured the coldest blast of air I'd ever felt. Like A/C channelling air from the North Pole. It chilled me to the core. My legs weakened. I couldn't have resumed running if I wanted to—but I didn't want to. An inexplicable sense of necessity held me there. This encounter—whatever it was or meant—must happen, I thought, though I can't say if the thought originated in my mind or arrived there from an external source. The window framed a gaunt, pale face, shaded by a black hat. Eyes like coals settled their gaze on me, surveyed me, scanned me, assessed me, measured me, and judged me. The driver's observation ambushed my sense of self, penetrated to my bones. Everything around us came to a dead halt. No birds passed overhead. No noise reached my ears from any of the homes where earlier I'd heard yard tools buzzing and voices talking. No cars entered the street. No one came or went from any of the houses.

Whatever criteria the driver applied to me, he ultimately appeared satisfied. He withdrew into the darkness inside his vehicle, rolled up the window, and drove away, leaving me shaken and barely able to keep upright on my wobbling legs. The car reached the next corner, a T-intersection that required it to turn left or right. Instead, it simply continued forwards toward a house—then vanished into thin air before reaching the opposite kerb.

The second it disappeared, my legs gave out, dropping me to the ground.

Life and sound rushed back to the block. Birds chirped. Across the street, a paunchy man pushed a growling mower onto his lawn. An ordinary car backed out of a drive and rolled by, the mother and daughter inside glancing at me with curious expressions.

Finding the strength to stand, I resumed my walk home, shocked, and determined to force my father to answer my questions. The moment he laid eyes on me, his face paled. He already knew what had happened. He saw it in me. A change invisible to myself, perhaps to anyone other than my father — but he saw it, and he *knew*, and I demanded he explain it.

Chapter Ten

From The East End Chronicle, *"Police Blotter," July 1, 2014*

Reports of a possible wildfire led police to the woods behind Sam's Electronics in the strip mall at 72 Bogue Avenue, Riverhead, where they found evidence of a migrant camp. The isolated stanch of trees and wild growth, which abuts the Peconic River on the south, has become a gathering place for migrant workers and the homeless. Police found two tents, three sleeping bags, makeshift shelters erected from tarpaulins hung on rope strung between tree trunks, food waste, discarded clothing, a shopping cart full of empty cans, and other evidence of inhabitation, in a state of ruin described by a responding officer as resembling "a trailer park after a twister." No sign of the inhabitants was found. The smoke that initiated the investigation came from a smoldering campfire, which police extinguished.

A Riverhead Police cruiser occupied the spot closest to the front door of Riverhead Canoe and Kayak Rentals. A bell above the door rang as I entered. Officer Nowak stood at the counter, chatting with the owner. As the door closed behind me, their conversation died. Mr. Owens stared daggers at me.

"That's him," he said. "That's the lying bastard."

"Okay, easy, Mr. Owens. I'll take it from here." The cop straightened and greeted me, his hands hooked on his belt in a confident pose. "Mr. Benjamin Keep?"

My body tensed. My mouth dried up. I cleared my throat. "Yes, that's me."

"Thank you for coming. We need your help pinning down some facts about a recent death." He pulled a notebook from his pocket and flipped it open. "Did you and Ms. Annetta Maikels rent two kayaks, paddles, and life jackets from this establishment the day before yesterday?"

"Yes, we did," I said.

"You used them to travel along the Peconic River?"

"That's right."

"Did you return them to this establishment, per the rental agreement?"

"No, we didn't."

The questions continued, rehashing everything we'd already covered with the owner and other information, such as where we lived. I gave the address of my family home in Hicksville, still my official residence. Soon enough, we reached a turning point in the conversation. Although Mr. Owens seemed intent on melting me with his stare, Officer Nowak struck me as cool and reasonable. I gambled on the accuracy of my impression and decided to hew as close to the truth as possible rather than double down on our lie about the kayaks drifting away.

"So, you're saying you didn't lose the kayaks. You returned from hiking and found them smashed and broken?"

"That's right."

"Why would you lie about that?"

"We had no idea what had happened to them. We were afraid we'd be blamed for it. We didn't mind paying to replace them, but what if Mr. Owens reported us for destruction of property? We'd have trouble with the police over something we didn't do. It was so weird to find them cracked apart. Kids, we guessed, but it would take a lot of strength, maybe even sledgehammers or something, to break them up. That scared us. We wanted to get out of there. What if there were violent people around? We didn't want any trouble. We figured as long as we paid up, no harm, no foul."

"That's an interesting perspective. It didn't occur to you that by not reporting possible violent people, you placed others in danger?" Officer Nowak said.

I faltered only for a second before replying, but Nowak's expression altered subtly. He had caught my lie or at least found a thread upon which he could pull.

"No, I guess it didn't occur to us," I said.

"Uh-huh. Did you see anyone else around the area where you went hiking?"

Men in black suits who traveled with folding lawn furniture.

"Not really. A car went by."

"Did you know you were trespassing on private property?"

"Not at first. We didn't really see the house from the water. Once we saw it, we figured it was abandoned because it looked ready to fall over. We didn't think we were bothering anyone."

"No harm, no foul, again?"

"I guess."

"Listen, Mr. Keep. I appreciate you coming here and answering my questions, but I think you're holding something back. As Mr. Owens told you on the phone, which he wasn't supposed to do, we found a body with your kayaks. We're seeking leads. I feel like you might be hiding something. I can bring you down to the precinct for a detective to question you. We can bring in Ms. Maikels too. Or you can level with me and tell me what you're holding back."

"Who is it that died?" I said.

"Answer my questions first, please."

"Was it a migrant worker?"

Mr. Owens snorted, and said under his breath, "Of course, it was."

Officer Nowak glared at him. "Shut up, Teddy."

"Oh, come on, now. Those people don't belong here," Mr. Owens said. "You should be clearing them out. I bet it was a mob of them that smashed my kayaks."

"Really, Teddy? Why would they do that? Give me one good reason, and I'll listen."

Mr. Owens's frowned, shook his head, then turned to paperwork on the counter.

"Officer Nowak, tell me this much, did you find the whole corpse?" I said.

Nowak reluctantly shook his head.

"So, okay, I'll level with you. My fiancé and I were investigating the Peconic River Monster. We kayaked down to 4 Estuary Drive to check out sites where people reported the monster then snooped around that abandoned house. The man who lived there saw the monster. He might've been researching it too before he vanished. Want to know what really happened to our kayaks? The Peconic River Monster destroyed them while we rummaged through old books inside the house. That's the only thing I'm holding back. You can see why I would. No one was dead when we left there. We would've reported it if there was. I bet the monster dragged a migrant into the river and left it in the kayak debris later. What does your crime scene assessment show about when the body wound up there? If you've got a window for time of death, I'll bet it's after we left, which I can prove with my Uber records and our time here settling up with Mr. Owens. Or do you think we killed him?"

Nowak scowled. "Whether you killed someone or not, Mr. Keep, doesn't mean you're not linked to the crime."

"Have you seen the 2008 police report for that house, when a neighbor reported a break-in there? Maybe there are other reports like it between then and now?"

Officer Nowak's expression told me I'd struck a nerve. He sighed and flipped his notebook closed. "You expect me to put a crackpot story like that in my report?"

I didn't overlook that he hadn't said "expect me to believe that" and took hope he might know enough to recognize the unusual circumstances of the migrant's death.

"I'm only telling you what you wanted to know. I could've stuck to the story I told Mr. Owens. All that damage could've happened after we lost the kayaks. They floated away, beached themselves, some kids found them, and wrecked them. You asked me not to keep any information from you."

Nowak stared at me for several seconds, making up his mind, then handed me a business card and instructed me to keep in touch if I thought of anything else. As I turned for the door, Mr. Owens called me back to the counter.

"Hey, we haven't finished settling up yet," he said. "You lied to me!"

Nowak shook his head and waved a hand. "Enough, Teddy. You got your money to replace the gear and then some. This guy doesn't owe you anything more."

Mr. Owens sputtered for a moment then frowned and shrugged.

I left the shop, hopped in my car, and drove away, noticing Nowak on the other side of the glass door, watching me go. I should've driven straight back to Malik's and picked up working where I'd left off, but an idea nagged at me. I turned another direction and headed to 4 Estuary Drive.

The private cul-de-sac welcomed me with silence, a weird brittleness in the air, as if an invisible bubble surrounded me, the house, its yard, the riverbank, fragile enough it might shatter any moment. Loosened plywood lay where I'd left it on the ground. The opening beyond gaped black and threatening. Dry grass and weeds crunched underfoot.

The river came into view around the side of the house. I tracked to the backyard, to where Annetta and I had stashed the broken watercraft. Police tape hung from tree trunks, cordoning off a wide patch of the bank. Nothing remained. The body removed to the morgue, I assumed, and the kayak debris gathered for evidence. The river looked sheer and glassy, hardly a ripple upsetting its placidity. On a whim, I turned to the water and shouted "Hello!" at the top of my lungs. My voice seemed to fade, flat and lifeless. No echo returned.

Circumventing the police tape, I roamed along the bank until I found what I sought.

Footprints, mostly hidden under fallen pine needles. So easy to miss if you weren't looking for them, and the cops had no reason to do so. Gently brushing away the needles revealed a clear trail up the bank toward where the body had been found. I traced it, careful not to step on any of the prints, and took pictures on my phone as I progressed, lamenting that I hadn't brought my camera. The prints led me to the police tape barrier, where I stopped. They resembled no animal tracks I knew. They combined long, claw-like toes with wide, scaly webbing, the imprints so clear, they displayed individual scales and cracks in the nails. Crouching, I placed one hand on the earth beside the deepest print and snapped a photo, estimating the size of the foot at twice the size of my hand.

Circling around the crime scene, I picked up the trail. It led to the house. The prints faded as the soil grew harder, dryer, and thicker with weeds. I walked back to the bank, scanning every branch and tree trunk, until I discovered the prize I sought.

A tuft of hide clung to the protruding stump of a birch branch long ago trimmed away, leaving a two-inch, splintery finger against which the creature must have scraped on its path. I photographed it from every angle, used my hand again to establish scale, then slid my phone away and found a suitable twig with which to lift the specimen. Comprised mostly of coarse hairs sprouting from a scaly patch of dead skin, it also bore a handful of small, iridescent feathers. A surreal mix of armadillo hide, duck down, and otter hair. I wrapped it in a handkerchief and carried it with me.

Officer Nowak leaned against the hood of my car, waiting when I rounded the house. His police cruiser sat parked behind my vehicle. I shoved the specimen into my pocket to hide it.

"Interesting move, Mr. Keep, coming straight to a crime scene you say has nothing to do with you." He carried a manila folder tucked under one arm, which he slid free and slapped against his hand. "Not really the thing to do if you want to appear innocent."

"I said I had nothing to do with the migrant death," I hedged. "Totally different than the location itself. You already know we were here."

"Looking for your monster again?" Nowak shifted his weight, straightened, and approached me. "Find anything?"

"Not really."

Nowak grinned. "Right."

He extended his arm, offering me the folder, which I took.

"I grew up out here, Mr. Keep. My family goes way back. You think I think you're a nutjob making up stories about monsters because you're bored, delusional, or covering up something. All those possibilities occurred to me, and I haven't yet put them to rest. Except I see another possibility too — that says there might really be a monster in these waters. I won't try to explain. I won't *ever* report it that way. I'd be laughed off the job if I did, and I like my job. But I've heard the stories. Growing up here, most kids hear them, and most dismiss them. They're incredible, but they're few and far between. More than that, they're boring. Forgettable. Somebody saw a weird thing in the river. It never hurts anyone. It never does any harm. Except maybe once, and that time matters to me. How can I rule out — if it harmed one person — that it didn't harm others? You've been investigating already, so I'll give you the benefit of the doubt that you know how shallow the Peconic River is, how ridiculous it is to think it hides some kind of Loch Ness monster. I mean, at least over in Scotland, that lake is like, what, 800 feet deep and murky as hell? Something could really hide in there. But not here, no. Except..." Nowak trailed off and tapped the folder in my hands. "...here we got too many loose ends for me to ignore that one, wonky possibility. Not the Riverhead Police, mind you. Not the *East End Chronicle*. They ignore it just fine. It's only me here, one guy who's seen some weird shit speaking to another."

Opening the folder revealed a stack of photocopied police reports. I flipped through them until I realized what they had in common. Disappearances and corpses around the Peconic River area, migrant workers and teens with criminal records. The kind of people no one much noticed when they vanished.

"Have you seen this thing yourself?"

"Not me, no, and, frankly, I don't want to. If there's something weird in the river, I hope it stays submerged forever or finds its way to the ocean and leaves us behind," Nowak said. "Never saw anything around here that didn't belong, but my grand uncle did. Daune Sadowksi. Maybe you came across him in your research. He was one of the few documented sightings."

"Yes, I know. I interviewed his high school girlfriend."

"Yeah, she still lives around here. I keep an eye on her. I'd bet she doesn't know the whole story. My grandmother told it to me when I was kid. Her brother was never the same after he saw a monster in the river, and months later he crashed his car and died. After graduating high school, he kind of drifted. Odd jobs, no direction. The monster obsessed him. He lost sleep over it. My grandmother believed he was fleeing something that night, speeding—from a monster, his own demons? Who the hell knows? Maybe you can figure it out. Knowing there's really a monster out there—or there isn't—would mean something to my family."

I closed the folder and pulled the specimen from my pocket.

"I found this by the crime scene. Footprints too. It's evidence. We can share it. Set up watch. If the monster came here before, it'll come again."

Nowak eyed the crumpled handkerchief in my open hand. He unfolded it, touching it as little as possible, then stared at the patch of hide with a mix of awe, confusion, and terror. Sweat peppered his brow. I held my breath, hoping for him to join me. Instead, he wrapped the thing up, closed my fingers over it, and shook his head.

"I don't want to see," he said. "I'm a town cop. This shit's above my paygrade. I've helped you as much as I can for now, but you've got my card. Keep this to yourself unless you learn anything interesting about my grand uncle. Otherwise, nice to meet you, and good luck with… whatever."

He walked to his cruiser. I watched him pull out of the cul-de-sac onto River Road then got into my car, dropping the folder and specimen on the passenger seat. After a long look at the house, I felt certain I'd missed some clue or other obvious thing. Too much information swirled around my thoughts, the police reports increasing the chaos sown by

Burgess's jumbled research and writings. A wealth of documented facts that added up to nothing more than a good story.

What if that's all there was here?

Chapter Eleven

From the papers of Reginald Burgess, possible chapter of Natura Occulta, Volume Two, *unpublished. Reprinted here from a notebook marked "The Codes of My Ancestors."*

Stepping stones stretched behind me, rearranging themselves in my mind as my understanding of their path changed and expanded. My father's work taking him so often into the Outback or other remote locations. My mother's sudden health decline, followed by a prolonged state of limbo while she languished, incapacitated, before she succumbed. My affinity with nature, especially plants. From age five, I kept a vegetable garden in the backyard and tended the shrubs and flowers around our house; I climbed trees not only for adventure, but to examine their bark, branches, leaves, and blossoms. What seemed random and instinctive in the moment now struck me as cultivated and purposeful. Instead of a route of evolution and exploration as I engaged with the world and grew, I saw the trail of my life directed, manipulated, guided by an invisible hand. One that had deftly shaped my father's life too.

After my encounter with the man in the black car, after the "change" my father perceived in me, we returned to the secret water.

My father planned the trip with a level of precision and specificity that I assumed had preceded our first venture too, but he hadn't included me in the process then. Too young, I reckon. This time, he taught me what I came to think of as the "calculations of the mystery." The weighing and measuring of dates, weather records, lunar cycles, air-quality projections, even sunspot activity, and countless other factors in selecting the day most likely to provide our best opportunity to see the monster. The creature, my father explained, dwelt in a different mode of probability than us. Always present, but not always part of our shared environment. This meant sometimes we might see and interact with it, while at other times in the same location, we might not perceive it.

My father's analytical mind, comfortable with how numbers mapped and represented invisible workings of the world around us, helped him understand. My mind preferred the organic, the cellular, the tangible. Soil in my hand. Grass underfoot. The aroma of flowers in my nose. We worked through the calculations over and again until I mastered the process if not the principles. I couldn't explain the inner workings of a car, but I could drive one well enough.

Once we settled on the optimal date, we collected the necessary gear.

During the several weeks we waited, my father said no more about it. We talked only about his regular work, my school, the weather, and countless other quotidian topics, all grating my urgency for the date to come. To this day, I've no idea how my father so fully compartmentalized his apprehension and curiosity during the in-between times. Perhaps his scientific mind simply couldn't fret a thing before it occurred. I sensed in him a reluctance to share his secrets. Reluctance outweighed by necessity. By duty. He wanted a different life for me, but he couldn't bring himself to provide it.

The day of our planned trip, we departed before dawn.

I've withheld the date on purpose, as I've withheld the location. The fewer people who know either, the better for the secret my father bestowed to me, for the creature in the water. Safer, too, for anyone who might seek it out unarmed with the knowledge to do so safely.

Leaving our Land Rover at the same location, we bypassed our previous campsite and hiked the trail beyond our observation point from that long-ago night. In places, the trail succumbed to rock spills and overgrowth, impossible to trace for anyone who didn't already know it. How far we hiked, I won't record. My father is long gone now. No one but me needs such details, but their usefulness has faded since I left Australia. That secret place still exists, but it no longer serves the same purpose.

I knew immediately when we reached our destination. The air felt charged and damp, and the hairs on my arms stood up. Sounds dimmed. The sunlight brightened and baked across my face. The dirt sank underfoot with a rubbery consistency. I recognized none of the plants growing in the area. They all looked familiar, as if I should know them, but altered. Wrong-colored flowers. Too many or too few blades on the leaves. Corkscrewed stems. The insects buzzing around them looked wrong too. Bluish bees. Transparent dragonflies the length of my middle finger. A twelve-legged spider ignited a shudder of revulsion. I crouched for a closer look, but it scurried under a rock. Even the stones seemed different, with a faint iridescence to them.

My father continued a few steps farther then stopped and placed his hand on my chest to halt me. Instead of speaking, he gestured. *Listen.*

Only the mélange of odd sounds.

I shook my head, shrugged.

He gestured. *Close your eyes.*

Shutting off my sight collated random noises into a persistent thrum with a cardiac rhythm. I fell into it and swayed. My father gripped my arm, bracing me.

A voice joined the quilt of sound. High-pitched and animal. Full of hunger and need.

I snapped my eyes open. Pushing past my father, I rushed up the trail, ignoring his shouts to slow down, wait for him, take care, keep my head. That animal cry hooked my soul, irresistible.

When I reached the top of a low ridge, I halted, stunned by what awaited on the other side.

The water creature from that night lay curled in a billabong no more than thirty meters away.

It lifted its fierce head, tusks gleaming in the sunlight.

Nestled against its elongated body, tucked between its legs, cozied in the folds of its tail, lay half a dozen eggs the size of truck tires. From one of them, its shell cracked, liquid contents spilling to the earth, protruded a miniature of the creature, still glistening with egg fluid, its mouth wide, crying for attention. Its tiny tusks quivered.

"Bonza, Reg, you heard it clearer than I ever did at your age," said my dad when he caught up to me. "Like it drilled right into your brain."

"Not my brain, Dad," I said, unable to look away from the hatchling. It stirred a million unfamiliar emotions. I struggled to make sense of them. "My soul."

"Aye, yeah, I guess so," he said.

"What is it?"

"Well, Reg, my lad, meet the ol' Bunyip."

Chapter Twelve

"What the hell is a bunyip?" I said.

Annetta grinned. "You're so cute when you don't know something."

"Aw, thanks." I blew her a sarcastic kiss across Malik's kitchen table. "You've heard of this thing?"

"Oh, yeah." Annetta poured the last of a bottle of pinot noir into her glass then sipped it, taking her time, making me wait, teasing me. "It's an Australian cryptid. Legends go back hundreds of years to before Europeans reached the continent. It lives in or near water in wild places. It's big enough to drag people off to their death, which it has done a fair few times over the years, if you believe the folk tales. Big teeth. Fierce. Hairy. Shaggy. Stealthy. Picture an ox or a horse, but aquatic. Or a bull seal. That's one theory about the legend. Leopard seals wandering inland from the shore. They were quite the talk of Oz in the 1800s, but there hasn't been a serious report of an encounter for so long, I'd have guessed the chances of a real one ever showing up were about the same as finding a genuine mermaid. They're the stuff of kiddie books now."

"It sounds like a mammal," I said. "Like an overgrown otter or a seal."

"Hmm-mm, it sure does," said Annetta.

"Burgess writes about its eggs. Mammals don't lay eggs."

"It's Australia, hon. They build 'em different Down Under. You never heard of a platypus?"

"The bunyip is a giant platypus?"

"Ben, dear, sweetheart, if this thing is real, it'll be the biggest zoological discovery in fifty years. Don't ruin it with dumb questions."

"Ouch." I mimed an injured heart.

"Australia is home to marsupials, platypuses, and a bumper share of the world's deadliest critters. Normal rules don't apply."

"Long Island isn't Australia. How'd it get here? Is it the Paul Hogan of cryptids? *Oy, Bigfoot, you call that a foot? That's not a foot. This is a foot!*"

"Paul who? What the hell are you talking about?"

"Paul Hogan. Crocodile Dundee?"

"Doesn't ring a bell." Annetta shook her head.

"Next you'll tell me you've never seen a Peter Weir movie or listened to Men at Work."

"Let's not change the subject."

"Fine. So that thing we saw down the well, the one that probably smashed our kayaks, and killed who knows how many migrants over the years—that's a bunyip?"

"Maybe. Or maybe Reg Burgess only believed it was."

"Another possibility, true."

"The question is what do we do about it? A real-life bunyip would set the zoological world on its head."

"You're not thinking about capturing it."

"What better proof than the thing itself?"

I rose and walked to the kitchen window, once smashed in by a tree trunk thrown by a Bigfoot, still so fresh, Malik hadn't painted the new window frame yet. The glass reflected my face. I tried to see through it, across the yard, into the edge of the Pine Barrens that abutted Malik's property. Peering into the darkness, knowing it held so many secrets yet discovered, pieces of a puzzle so vast and difficult to comprehend, the obscuring void often seemed like a comfort. Somewhere in that yard, invisible to me, stood a shark cage decked out like a garden gazebo, a relic from when Malik, Annetta, and I tried to catch one of those secrets and failed. Like grasping a mist that, by chance, forms a shape that disintegrates before your hand even comes close to it.

"It's a serious question, Ben. What have we got to lose?"

I spun on my heels, frowned, then marched into the living room where I'd stored the file folder from Officer Nowak. I brought it to the kitchen and slapped it down on the table.

"Our lives." I took my seat, opened the file, then lifted the first page, and read. "Corpse of a middle-aged, Hispanic man separated at the waist by apparent crushing force." Flipped to the next page. "A Caucasian man in his early thirties bisected at the waist." The next. "Upper torso hanging from a low tree branch as if hurled there. The pelvis and legs lay at the water's edge." Another. "The victim's upper body lay face down in the water on the bank, legs and pelvis beside him. The toes of his left foot abutted his forehead." One more. "The decapitated corpse of a middle-aged Hispanic man, which spent several weeks in the water. Shall I go on to the next page and the next? If a bunyip did all this, what makes you think we can capture one without winding up chomped in two?"

"We'll know what we're looking for. We won't get caught by surprise."

"That thing did a damn good job surprising us in Reg Burgess's basement. Did it smash our kayaks to warn us? To strand us? How intelligent is a bunyip?"

"Good question." Annetta's brow furrowed as she slipped into deep thought. "I don't know how smart they are. I was thinking of it as an animal governed by instinct. Some Aboriginal myths regard it as divine creature, a beast of the Dreamtime. Maybe it's more than a mere animal. Do those reports say where those men died?"

"No. They only say where their bodies were found. Some might have died in the same place, but it sounds like whatever the thing is, it might've held onto them for a while, moved them around. Maybe like alligators stash their prey to decompose and soften before they feed."

"Yeah, maybe. Okay, here's what we do…"

We cleared the kitchen table, washed the dishes, stored the leftovers, then moved to the living room to try Annetta's idea. We unfolded a map of Long Island from the travel atlas I carried in my car. My father had given it to me when I first got my driver's license. It had lived in every car I'd owned, almost entirely unused due to GPS apps, but comforting to have. Annetta and I marked the sites where bodies had been found along the Peconic River, drawing red circles to memorialize them, until we noticed not so much a pattern but a tendency of geography and seasons.

The deaths began in spring, around April, and lasted until November. Almost no reports through the winter. The one outlier in Nowak's files, a January death, looked more like a boating accident than a bunyip attack. A drunk celebrating New Year's too hard alone on his boat, fell off and wound up bisected by the propeller. We left that one off our map. The deaths ran from fewest out east near Flanders Bay to the most, moving west, growing in number as we followed the lines to Peconic Lake and 4 Estuary Drive. Most years there were no deaths at all that fit the pattern, but in the "on" years, bodies washed up at half a dozen spots along the lake and river, all in the most isolated areas. The victims were all migrants and drifters except for two teen pushers whose deaths remained overlooked for almost a year. People figured they'd skipped town.

"We've got one likely death this year right at Burgess's old house." I marked a red circle on the map. "One near Flanders Bay and two more in between going by Nowak's info. Nothing in the past three years. That makes this an "on" year. Why the gaps? Two or three years. One as long as five starting in 2000. If it kills to eat, what's it chowing on in the years no deaths are reported?"

"It's hibernating," Annetta said. "Or it has a slow metabolism and rarely needs to feed, but when it does it eats its fill. When you're big enough to bite people in two feeding infrequently would go a long way to helping you keep a low profile."

"An evolutionary advantage," I said. "Doesn't explain why it binges every few years."

"Its metabolism increases in those years. It requires greater nutrition."

"Why? What would cause that?"

"Increased activity. A crisis. Or… oh, shit," Annetta said.

"What? What is it?"

"Reproduction."

"You mean its laying eggs those years?"

"That's exactly what I mean."

"There could be more bunyips out there. No. There *should* be more. All those years of feeding and laying eggs, at least some of its offspring would've survived. One weird creature hiding out here, okay, maybe, I can kinda see it. Two or three? Or more? There just isn't enough water and land to hide that many."

"I agree with you, but nature is hard on the young, especially those hatched outside their natural habitat. Chicks hatched by hens survive better than those hatched in incubators. If Burgess brought this thing here as a pet, it might not have what it needs to reproduce successfully. It might lay infertile eggs."

"Right, what about a mate? Doesn't it take two to, you know, tango?"

"Usually, but not every species reproduces that way. It might be asexual. Might even eat its own young if they're born unhealthy. If the mother senses they won't survive in the environment, she might devour them. Conservation of resources and competition reduction drive some nasty behaviors in the animal kingdom. Maybe that's what fuels the long periods of inactivity."

"That's utterly horrifying."

My stomach flip-flopped at the idea of that tusk-faced beast at the bottom of the well snapping up its young the moment they cracked their shells. The poor little bastards. I couldn't help but picture them like cartoon puppies or seals with wide eyes, sweet faces, and adorable whiskers. The mother, their executioner.

"Nature ain't pretty all the time, sweetheart," Annetta said.

"I don't think Burgess brought it here as a pet, though. That doesn't feel right. There's too much more going on with his father, the secret calculations, a duty passed down through generations."

Pulling the map onto her lap, Annetta scanned the marks along the river. "There's something else, Ben. If it *has* been laying eggs, then it has a nest, one it goes back to, like the place in Burgess's notes. A home where it feels safe."

"The basement on Estuary Drive. That sure looked like a nest."

"It did, but I don't think that's it. Burgess's description of the nest made it sound like a special place, a place outside regular reality. Somewhere between Flanders Bay and 4 Estuary Drive, there's a secret place where it hides. We have to find where it is, ideally before anyone else dies."

"How do we do that?"

"We crack Burgess's code. What did he call it? Calculating the mystery? We do that and we'll know where and when to look."

Chapter Thirteen

From the papers of Reginald Burgess, possible chapter of Natura Occulta, Volume Two, *unpublished. Reprinted here from a collection of writings on the back of student test papers from Botany 101, marked "Appetites."*

My father died. My father vanished. My father went away.

My father took a holiday from which he never returned. My father slipped through the cracks. My father never existed in the first place, except as a legend, a myth, an unfulfilled wish in my mind.

By the year I graduated from college, it all seemed true.

My father's absence weighed on me as if I'd lived my whole life without him despite him always being there for me while I grew up, mentoring me, teaching me, leading me, always serving up a laugh to raise my spirits. I didn't resent him for leaving, disappearing, or dying, whatever the case. My mother's death taught me the ephemera of life and family. I harbored no anger. He didn't choose to leave—that I firmly believe. He had no choice. I held no bitterness over how far too early our inevitable parting—and my orphaning—came.

I felt only disappointment, sadness, and shock.

I missed him. I wished I could share my accomplishments with him. Share a laugh. Share a beer.

Share one more night watching stars from the back porch, wondering upon what mysteries and secrets their light fell.

When I entered university, Dad resumed travelling for work. He took assignments all around the continent and spent more time in the bush than he had since before my birth. My third year, he left for an assignment in the region of the billabong trail that led to the bunyip.

He never returned.

No word ever came. No reports of his gear or vehicle—or body—found.

He stepped into the throat of the world, and the world swallowed him.

Like a black car traversing an intersection into invisibility.

Crossing an invisible line on a dirt trail that sets your hair on end.

I searched for him as best I could. His company reported his last known location at his final check-in. From there, he could've gone in a dozen directions, one of which only I knew led to the secret water. I followed them all, hoping for some clue or hint, seeking a place where his presence still echoed. I even hoped I might walk into a local watering hole and find him drunk at the bar, too knackered to make his way home. Each time, I found myself drawn back to the secret water, to the long and overgrown trail. I visited it several times. Scoured the earth and brush for a dropped or discarded item that spoke to his presence. I found nothing but rock, sand, spinifex, and insects. I stopped myself always at the fringe of crossing into that strange zone onto the billabong trail, where he'd taken me to see the bunyip.

My father had warned me not to set foot there at the wrong time.

I clung to that caution out of fear for my safety as much as to honour my father's wishes.

Black cars stalked me. In the middle of nowhere, my Land Rover the only vehicle on the road for an hour, one would abruptly appear in my rearview mirror, as if spat out of thin air, and follow me only to vanish when I took my eyes off the mirror for a moment. They roamed my neighbourhood around the old family home, where I still lived. I spent less time there, favouring the uni lab, where I pursued research, transforming my childhood green thumb into expertise in botany. My work took me around the country. Rain forests. Deserts. Botanical gardens. The Great Barrier Reef to study marine plants. Everywhere, black cars. Always at a distance, never intrusive. None ever approached me, window rolled down, for the driver to stare. Still, I received their message. They were watching. Waiting, I suppose, to see how I would fill my father's shoes or if I would at all.

I'd already begun the calculations he'd taught me, charting the next safe date to venture out to the bunyip's billabong for one last attempt to learn my dad's fate, to understand my family's history with the creature. I charted the intimidating list of variables. Weather. Soil pH. Star positions. Magnetic waves. Sunspot activity. All the things Dad showed me. When the day came, I arrived at the secret water place at midday. The high sun cooked the earth and me as I trammeled along the trail. I passed familiar spots, reached the point of no return, hesitated there, knowing I could still turn back and leave all this, forget the strange experiences of my youth, my mysterious birthright, and live whatever life I chose.

Two more steps, though, would stitch all that forever into the fabric of my life.

I took those steps.

The weird zone jolted my body the way it had my first time there.

I followed the trail, recalling my father's path.

I reached the same ridge and looked into the billabong.

At initial glance, I mistook it for empty. The vegetation, which despite my years of field study and research, remained unidentifiable to me, lay lush and overgrown down to the water line of the bunyip's billabong nest. Then plant fronds rustled, and the bunyip's pendulous head rose from the green. It lay stretched along the bank, sickly, exhausted, and heartbroken. I don't know how I read that last emotion in its eyes — but I did. I had no doubt about it. The way you read the worried eyes of a devoted dog when you're leaving it, I suppose. The bunyip looked abused. Traumatized. The worse for wear. Patches of fur and feathers had dropped from its hide, exposing the scales beneath. It lifted its head a few inches higher, flashing an angry, frightened expression at me, before it decided I posed no threat and lowered its head to its paws again.

All around it lay the fragments of cracked, citrine shells, floating in gooey, orange puddles of amniotic ooze, remnants of a dozen hatched eggs.

I peered up and down the bank, in the water, in the trees, seeking its young.

Nothing — until a short, high-pitched cry came from the other side of a low hill behind the bunyip. Following my heart, I rushed down the ridge, splashed across the water, which reached my waist at its deepest, then dashed across to the other bank. Passing the wearied bunyip, I feared perhaps I'd made a fatal blunder, and it would pounce, trap me behind its tusks, break me in half, drown me. It didn't. Either it remained indifferent to me — or, as I believe I saw in the narrowing of its eyes — it thanked me for taking the action it lacked the strength to do.

I scaled the bank and subsequent hill. At the top, a dry, brown meadow opened before me, cut through only by a slender dirt road. A black car sat there. Back doors and trunk open. The meadow stretched to an immeasurably distant horizon of sky the color of blue taffy. Like a postcard painting.

Two pale men in black suits stalked toward the car. Each dragged behind him a makeshift sled of black cloth, stuffed with newborn bunyips. The men paused and looked at me, their eyes invisible under their hat brims, their grins glinting in the strong light. Grins that turned my blood cold.

I bolted down the hill, struggling to keep my balance, then launched into the meadow.

I shouted for the men to leave the bunyips and explain themselves.

They ignored me. Their car grew farther away, not closer, with every step I took. My legs turned rubbery and weak, yet the men made steady progress, leaving me no chance to overtake them. At their vehicle, they loaded one sack of bunyip young into the boot, the other into the backseat. The boot and back doors slammed shut, seemingly on their own. The men slipped onto the front seat from either side, then the car drove.

Its engine hummed and its tyres spun without a sound, spewing a massive rooster comb of red dust into the air. It surged forwards on the dirt road. Suddenly, strength returned to my legs. I surged like a sprinter out of the gate, set foot on the dirt road, and saw the car — a single bunyip hatchling gaping out the back windscreen, half-hidden by the tinted glass — wink out of sight into an invisible elsewhere.

Despondent, I trekked back to the billabong.

Had my father come here alone, only for the men who drove black cars to carry him away? Had he fallen prey to another danger? Had the water dragged him under and swept him away?

I reached the billabong. The withered bunyip watched me with an expectant gaze. It shared my mood. Crushed by the theft of its young, I assumed, but another pain afflicted it.

Hunger.

Nurturing its hatchlings had drained it, left it weak. It needed to feed to restore itself. It tracked me with its eyes wherever I walked, locked onto me, worried at me with its expression. It expected me to provide it with a meal. I had no idea what bunyips ate. The billabong offered few morsels. If I left to gather food, I might not find the trail again. Not for weeks, at least, when it would properly converge with the billabong. I'd already done the calculations. Even if it survived without tucker that long, what could I bring to fill its belly? A cow?

The horror came first, then the memory—of a teenage boy in his boxer shorts on the bank of the water one moment, gone the next. My blood chilled when I finally understood what aspect of the family duty passed down generation to generation my father had left for me to learn for myself.

CHAPTER FOURTEEN

After hours of trying to piece together Reginald Burgess's code to calculate the mystery based on hints and clues in his writing, we gave up, exhausted, no closer to understanding his relationship to the bunyip. We contemplated packing everything away and returning to our normal lives. We had taken our investigation as far as possible and reached a dead end. We sat on Malik's back porch, drinking wine, staring into the Pine Barrens, daring them to show a glimpse of the mystery. The longer I looked into those woods, though, the more certain I became that those mysteries would never manifest among them again. They had served their purpose when they contributed to me, Annetta, and Malik solving the mysteries of the Montauk Monster. Now, they were just woods that held no more secrets to divulge. They had given us everything we needed.

Everything we needed.

"Where's the Keel book we took from Reg's bedroom?" I said.

"*Mothman Prophecies?*"

"Yeah."

"In the house, I guess..."

I went inside and searched everywhere but didn't find the book. I grew certain I'd left it behind in the cottage. I'd been skimming it, reading Reg's margin notes, finding them cryptic and obtuse. It had sat on the nightstand when the intruders woke me. I stepped back onto the porch.

"It's not here," I said. "I must've left it at the cottage."

Annetta squinted. "What's the big deal?"

"What if that's the piece we're missing to make sense of this?"

"I don't get it."

"Burgess's margin notes read like nonsense. He related things with no connection, mentioned irrelevant topics, and wrote nonsense words. If he wasn't a full-blown crackpot writing radio-signals-to-his-brain, stream-of-consciousness word salad, then what if those notes are the code key? His father's calculating the mystery process sounds complex and intricate. Could he memorize it and risk forgetting part of it? No. He didn't have an analytical mind like that. He had to have written it down."

"It sounds like a stretch," Annetta said.

"It's the last card we have to play."

Annetta agreed, and we rushed to the car, leaving our full wine glasses behind.

During the drive, a cloud of anxiety, fatigue, and pessimism stifled us to silence. If this gamble failed, we could go no further. My instinct proved true: I'd missed an obvious clue, only not at 4 Estuary Drive — or at least, no longer there. I'd scooped up that book out of nostalgia and curiosity, tossed it in with the rest of Burgess's ephemera, and overlooked its significance.

I turned the car at the corner for the cottage then slammed the brakes.

Flashing red-and-white lights and a flickering orange glow danced along the block.

Across the street from the cottage crowds of neighbors watched firefighters spray water as our borrowed home burned. Dense and threatening smoke billowed from the roof. Tongues of flame licked through heat-shattered glass, lashing out from the second-floor bedroom windows. I pulled as close as possible before a policeman blocked the way. Annetta and I exited the car and stared at the conflagration.

"Guess we're not getting that book," she said.

A sickening thought occurred to me: If we hadn't moved to Malik's we'd have been asleep in that blaze, very possibly burned to death. I hugged Annetta, needing to feel her close to me.

"That phone call saved our lives," I said. She didn't understand right away. "Malik or not, that call got us out of the cottage, or we'd have been asleep right there where the flames are the worst."

The realization brought tears to her eyes. Part of the cottage roof collapsed. A fiery whirlwind spit into the night sky. The gawkers gasped.

Annetta's phone rang. The name of her colleague, whose mother owned the cottage, appeared on the screen.

"Yes, yes, we're okay. We weren't inside when it started," she said, answering. "I'm so sorry. The whole place is going up."

She paced to our car and leaned against it. I roamed closer to the cottage and watched the place burn. What had ignited the flames? Had someone wanted us there when they sparked?

Down the block, a familiar figure caught my eye. A man in a black coat and hat.

He walked around the corner. I ran past the firefighters and the crowds and followed. He never walked so far ahead I lost sight of him. Around the next corner, down the next block, to the house that adjoined the cottage lot. More clustered neighbors watched the fire. Domingo, who lived behind us, stood in his driveway with a garden hose ready should the fire catch the fence between our yards. The Man in Black walked up the driveway. Domingo showed no sign of seeing him, as if he were invisible. Nor did he recognize me or my presence when I passed him.

I stood by the fence with the Man in Black. Heat reddened my face and started me sweating. Smoke tickled my throat and coated my nostrils. I unfolded a handkerchief from my pocket, pressed it to my face, and breathed through it.

"This neighborhood is a good one to raise a family," the Man in Black said.

"Why are you here? Did you start this fire?" I said.

"Firebugs go where they're not wanted. They break in where they don't belong. They leave little gifts to make you happy, then when you feel good, the fire starts."

"I don't understand," I said.

"We didn't take the box that day, but you left behind a thing from the box. Would you like it back?"

"A thing?" I said.

At 4 Estuary Drive, they'd packed their table and chairs, but left the bankers box with Burgess's notebooks and papers — and his copy of *The Mothman Prophecies*, which I'd tossed in with them.

"Do you want it? Answer fast, please."

"Yes, yes, I want it. Do you have it?"

The Man in Black rippled and quivered. A wave of heat passing between us, maybe. Maybe not. His pale, bony hand, shimmering in the firelight, reached into his pocket, and when he pulled it out, it clutched a scorched copy of *The Mothman Prophecies*.

"We still can't give you a ride," he said. "We're not going your way."

I riffled the browned, brittle pages, skimming Burgess's margin notes. When I looked up, the Man in Black was gone.

"Hey, Ben! What the hell? Get away from there, man!" Domingo now saw me. He waved furiously for me to move back from the fence. "There's nothing you can do. That fence could go up any minute. Stay clear, okay. I gotta make sure the fire doesn't spread over here."

I left Domingo and walked back to our car, where over the phone, Annetta comforted her friend over the loss of the cottage, reassuring him we hadn't done anything to start the fire, or anything that might void the insurance. She flashed me a look as I approached. I held up the book.

Mid-sentence, she said, "Jordan, I've got to call you back," then ended the call. "How the hell?"

"Get in the car. I'll explain while we drive back to Malik's."

Chapter Fifteen

From the papers of Reginald Burgess, possible chapter of Natura Occulta, Volume Two, *unpublished. Reprinted here from a series of notes written in a pocket address book, marked "Nutritional Requirements of a Bunyip."*

Experiencing a series of shocks results in numbness. It accreted an invisible, hard shell around me to the point where the weird and unexpected no longer troubled me, but ordinary days teaching, researching, cleaning the house, or grocery shopping left me shaking with anxiety and unable to sleep. What the bunyip ate made a hard pill to swallow, but at least my father hadn't left me entirely without guidance about how to feed it. I discovered detailed notes and instructions hidden in his work papers, which I'd never thought to go through before I cleaned out his office to prepare our family home for sale. I don't blame him for hiding what I found, for wanting me to see it only after he departed, only after he would no longer have to look me in the eye and answer my questions. No one wants their son to see them as a rival to Ivan Milat, the infamous Backpack Murderer.

My father used his work trips into the bush to tend to the bunyip and find people no one would notice missing to feed it. The gruesome revelation marked the last of my father's secrets. I uncovered maps of his back country hunting routes, his criteria for choosing the bunyip's next meal, and his trial-and-error notes about the best ways to incapacitate a person for transport to the bunyip's billabong. Leaving me on my own to discover this facet of our family history made sense to me over time. Each generation's custodian had to make this choice for themselves. No father should obligate his son to play the part of a serial killer. No son should feel obligated to take on the role.

I could have walked away.

Maybe I should have.

Maybe I would have if I hadn't already fed the bunyip once. That first time at the billabong on my own, pity for the creature swayed me. I knew from my calculations that the billabong trail would remain open a few hours more. I cruised the area for a likely meal. If I didn't find one, I'd drive home and never come back. I won't share the details. Suffice it to say, I met a young man in a mentally compromised state who'd pulled to the roadside to relieve himself. My means of getting him into my car and persuading him to hike the billabong trail doesn't matter. All that matters is I succeeded. His eyes lit with awe when he saw the bunyip—then terror exploded across his face as the ravenous creature snared him behind its tusks. Thankfully, it submerged to complete its meal, sparing me a gruesome sight.

With the window of access closing, I fled the billabong, frightened of getting trapped there.

On the drive home, I roughed out the calculations of mystery, and realized I had an eighteen-month reprieve before I need worry about the bunyip again. I had a choice to make, but in actuality, I'd already made it. As if on cue, a black car appeared in my rearview. I'd seen them around, here, there, and everywhere since my father vanished, like pop's old mates keeping an eye on me. They never came close, never showed their faces, but they let me know they were thinking of me.

What got under my skin most in those eighteen months were the Men Who Aren't There.

At first, I took them for partners to the men in black cars. I'd sense eyes watching me, looking over my shoulder, staring at me from across a road—I'd turn to look—and no one! Only the vaguest impression that I'd glimpsed some figure that instantly vanished when I looked. A human-shaped blur. So fleeting I found it easy to chalk it up to a trick of the light, my paranoia, my loneliness. None of these explanations stood the test of time. Especially not after the Men Who Aren't There started breaking into my house at night.

The first time, they bumped around my father's office. I cowered behind my locked bedroom door and called the police. They came fast, found no one, and told me it must've been a nightmare. The next time, I grabbed my camera and a cricket bat and went to confront them. When I opened the door to my father's office, they blinked out of existence. Silence. Stillness. My nerves gave out, and I flopped into my father's office chair. I sat there until dawn. They came a third time, all in the year and a half before I might access the billabong trail again. This time

I skulked outside my father's office and listened. They spoke nonsense words, voices muffled by the door, and thumped and banged around the office for nearly an hour. Then the door swung open on its own. I peered in, disoriented by the now-familiar, ephemeral glimpse of someone occupying a space that immediately appeared empty. I checked for signs of intruders, finding nothing at first, until I noticed among my father's papers an extra notebook identical to his other's but looking brand-new. Despite its appearance, my father's handwriting filled every page of it, but the ink looked fresh, the pages crisp, unlike the others.

I sat in my father's chair, read the notebook straight through, then rested my head on his desk, overcome by fear and the unwelcome realization that I must leave Australia.

Chapter Sixteen

Twilight draped the landscape in mystery.

Shadows deepened to crisp, utter black silhouettes, tricking my eyes into seeing holes in the world. Dark patches that looked deep enough to reach a hand into and grab something impossible. A cosmic magician pulling a not-a-rabbit-thing out of a hat.

Annetta and I sat on the bank of the Peconic River behind 4 Estuary Drive with a flannel blanket wrapped across our shoulders. Early spring weather meant no mosquitoes, but the warmth of the day fled with the sun. The air cooled. The breeze chilled us. The river's surface rippled with goose pimples. The quiet rejected us, as if nature had silenced itself in our presence, waiting for us to leave to renew its conversation. My arm around Annetta's back, I squeezed her shoulder.

"Everything's creepier in the dark," I said.

"This is worse than the dark," she said. "This feels… otherworldly."

"That's good, right? We didn't come here for the fresh air."

I lifted the camera from the ground at my side. Annetta smiled.

Burgess's *Mothman Prophecies* margin notes helped us crack enough of his code to calculate a night likely for the bunyip to appear — the last night for a long time if we'd done it right. His notes and the bits of Keel's writing to which they alluded combined with the few details Burgess had recorded directly, revealing enough of the formula for us to fill in the rest.

"Something's been bugging me," Annetta said.

"What's that?"

"The bunyip's victims were all loners and migrants. If it's responsible for all those deaths, it's smart enough to know not to attack people in pairs or groups. It knows enough to target people who won't be missed. People in the cracks of society. How can an animal tell all that?"

"Don't predators single out the weak and separate them from the herd?"

"Some, yeah, but this seems different. Targeted."

"Clever."

"Yeah, exactly."

"Or trained."

"Oh my god, Burgess *taught* it who to eat?"

"What are the chances of appropriate prey wandering by some Outback watering hole when the trail opened to let the bunyip into our world? Pretty slim, I'd imagine. Burgess made sure food arrived in the right place at the right time. From most of his writing, he seems like a decent guy, not a motivated psycho killer. Stepping into those shoes probably took a toll on him. Maybe he couldn't live with it so he decided to train the bunyip to do the work itself, how to choose safe meals, then brought him to a place where prey would be more plentiful."

"Ben, my love, I owe you an apology for ever putting that whacko's book in your hands."

"No, you don't. We'd be here one way or another. The Men in Black and the Men Who Aren't There are pulling our strings. We're proxies in their conflict. The Men Who Aren't There tried to confuse us then burn us to death. The Men in Black intervened and helped us. Honestly? I still don't know who the good guys are."

"Maybe there are no good guys," Annetta said.

"A sobering thought."

I shrugged out of the blanket and crept down the bank, camera raised, snapping shots of the sky bruised with orange-and-indigo streaks. The river appeared on my camera screen in stark hues. Turning around, I snapped a few photos of Annetta. I walked back, past our stakeout point, and shot photos of Burgess's house. The unstable tilt of its walls looked even more pronounced in the twilight.

A car growled by in the distance, probably on River Road.

No other sound filled the air.

I looked back to Annetta, who stood now and stared at the river.

"Why are we here?" I said.

Annetta walked to me, wrapping the blanket around herself against the cool night.

"To photograph the damn thing. If we can't capture it, we need some kind of proof."

"No, no, I mean, what are we really doing? Why do we care? Why are we trying to prove this thing exists at all? I think we're here for a different purpose. We have a role to play. Even if we prove bunyips are real along the way, who cares? It would be huge news, but whose lives would it change?"

"Ours. We'd be famous. We'd be rich. Part of history," Annetta said.

"How does that make our lives better? Money is nice, but we've spent the last few years keeping as low a profile as we can, trying to avoid the kind of people that going public with this will attract to our front door. Eventually, it would die down. We'd be left, maybe, with a little money in the bank. But would you give up your research or teaching? Do you expect me to give up my photography?"

"No, of course not," Annetta said. "We'll still be the same people."

"Right, so what's the point? Isn't it enough for us to know? The only life that will really change if we go public is the bunyip's. It might even be the end of the thing. Every amateur cryptozoologist will want some of the action. They'll flood the world with podcasts and reality TV shows like they have with Bigfoot. The difference is Bigfoot seems capable of taking care of himself. I can't stop thinking about what Burgess wrote, how the bunyip seemed heartbroken over its stolen young. Do you want to be part of that?"

Annetta's face pinched. Tears welled in her eyes.

"What if we're meant not to expose it but to protect it. The Men in Black took the young away. What could they want with them? I try to answer that question, and the most horrible ideas come to mind."

"Yeah, yeah, that bothers me too. We really have no idea what those goofballs are after."

"They've never stopped watching us. Like they knew we'd find ourselves at this point someday."

"Maybe. I don't have the answers, Annetta."

"I know you don't. Neither do I. But my gut says the right thing to do is to keep digging into this one, lock it down, and know for sure. Maybe it's enough for you and me to know the truth, and to hell with the rest of the world."

Annetta pulled me to her and kissed my lips. I let my camera hang from its strap, embraced her, and kissed her back. A shudder of terror ran through her when a strident, inhuman howl blasted the quiet and quivered the air. We hopped around and faced the river. A dead-black shape loomed out of the water. Emerging starlight glimmered in its eyes as its gaze locked on us. It howled again, mingling the call of a loon, the bark of a seal, and the roar of a lion. Sonic waves rattled me, tremored my bones. Annetta squeezed my hand so tight it hurt. I yanked it away from her, regaining my senses fast enough to lift my camera and take pictures.

The thing howled. My knees shook.

Sucking in a deep breath, I approached the bank, snapping shot after shot, ignoring Annetta, yelling at me to watch out. I reached the water's edge without lowering my camera, the shutter clicking, the lens spinning as my fingertips dialed the world into focus.

The creature howled again, so close I felt its breath on my face.

The odor of something monstrous, animal, and feral.

I lowered the camera and looked up at its bulbous head dangling from an oddly thin neck no more than five or six feet above me. Its neck raised it higher still, then the beast retreated into the river, lowered itself, submerged, and vanished.

I crumpled to a sitting position on the ground.

Annetta threw her arms tight around me. We held onto each other until we stopped shaking.

Another howl echoed through the night—muffled, from behind us inside Burgess's house.

I overcame my deep reluctance to ever set foot inside 4 Estuary Drive again and ran. Annetta jogged with me. We entered through the gaping hole in the front of the house. The thing howled again, trembling the walls and floors, sending trickles of dust and debris drizzling down around us. We hurried to the basement, following the echoes.

In the backroom that contained the well, dim light shimmered off water.

Annetta and I crept across the threshold. I held my camera at chest height and snapped pictures every few seconds, catching whatever I could. The bunyip lay curled in its nest. Its tail and the long latter part of its lithe body hung into the well. In the curve of its upper torso lay nine eggs big as watermelons. Eyes shimmering in moonlight filtering through cracks high in the compromised walls, the bunyip gazed at us. It opened its mouth, yawning, released a low-throated growl, then snapped its jaws shut.

Stretched to full length, the bunyip would've spanned ten to twelve feet long. A blend of slick, oily fur and delicate, glimmery feathers covered its scaly hide. Its four serpentine legs ended in webbed paws with gnarled talons like claws from a horror movie. What appeared at first as a head too large and pendulous for its wiry neck consisted mostly of thick fur and feathers, enhancing its ferocious, tusked appearance. An animal capable of learning and interacting with humans, like a dog or a horse, but only an animal—with an unfortunate diet.

I turned to face Annetta. A man stood behind her—then gone!

I spun around, searching, spotted him again on the other side of the well—him or another man, I couldn't be sure—but for less than a second. My eyes playing tricks. My imagination running off its rails. Like Reg Burgess once thought, except neither of those things provided the answer.

"We're not alone," I said.

"You see them too?" said Annetta.

"What do we do?"

"How the hell should I know?"

I never replied. The bunyip unleashed a howl so powerful the room shook visibly. Stone walls cracked and clattered. The floor caved into a sinkhole. Well-water flooded around us, plunging us into darkness. Annetta and I held each other's hand, terrified of parting. How long we jumbled in the cold water, I don't know, but then a light appeared, and we swam toward it.

Chapter Seventeen

From the papers of Reginald Burgess, possible chapter of Natura Occulta, Volume Two, *unpublished. Reprinted here from a manuscript written on the back of graph paper pages with contour maps drawn in pencil on the front, marked "Moving Day."*

One more hatching season then I must go. Six months.

I've arranged for employment halfway around the world in a place no one would ever think to look for the mythical bunyip. Who'd search for the Loch Ness Monster in a puddle? Who'd hunt the Yeti at a ski resort with slopes covered in artificial snow? It's the only advantage I can give myself, and it offers me opportunities to shake free of certain, distasteful obligations.

I cannot leave any clue for the Men Who Aren't There.

They come and go as they please. Sometimes they leave me… gifts, warnings, threats? I'm never sure how to interpret the oddities they deposit in my house. Not mine for much longer. I've got a buyer on the line, and we're close to a final deal. If the Men Who Aren't There come looking after I leave, will the new residents think the house is haunted? Maybe it'll give them a story to share with the neighbors. Once the papers are signed, I'll be long gone. It's a shame I can't take the bunyip itself with me. How could I ever manage it? My god! Imagine! Trying to ship such a thing via airplane or cargo liner. Even if I owned a boat and the skill to sail halfway around the globe, what would it eat in the weeks required to make the journey?

No, sadly, it must be this way, the only way. Like my father did to me, the bunyip must pass its burden to a new generation.

Anticipating its forlorn expression when I arrive at the billabong without a meal saddens me. I must get there early this time. I've mastered calculating the mystery, gained as much skill as my father if not surpassed him. I will cross the line on the Billabong Trail the moment access opens, do what must be done, then flee with my prize: A single bunyip egg, bound for a new world.

Chapter Eighteen

Hazy sun beat down.

Annetta lay beside me on the bank of a billabong pool.

A bunyip howl filled the air.

Motion and chaos erupted around us.

I sat up. Two Men in Black gathered the bunyip's eggs while struggling against interference from unseen figures. Or barely seen. The Men Who Aren't There. The bunyip wriggled, snapping its jaws on empty air, hoping to snag one of the near-invisible invaders. I grasped for my camera to photograph the action. My fingers found a smashed ruin. Our tumble through the well had left it cracked and crushed.

"Where are we?" Annetta said.

"Don't you recognize it?"

Annetta nodded. "I was hoping I was wrong. How the hell did we get here? This is like Patricia Sung's house all over again, a place outside the rules. Should we stop the Men in Black from taking the eggs?"

I stood and helped Annetta onto her feet. "It looks like they're trying to save them."

"I feel so helpless," she said.

"Then let's see if this is really the same place Reg wrote about."

I hiked several feet up a hill from the bank and gestured for Annetta to follow.

We climbed, pushed through brush, and reached the peak, out of breath, our soaked clothes clinging to us, radiating wisps of steam as the sun dried them. The hill provided a view onto an endless, sere meadow, stretching to a crayon-blue horizon. A dirt road ran through it, continuing far beyond the vanishing point. A familiar black car with blue-and-gold plates sat on it.

"Are we in… Australia?" Annetta said.

"I don't think so," I said. "This is the Bunyip's Billabong. A place outside Australia, outside our world. Reg must have changed where the door between here and our world exists."

"Moved it from Australia to Long Island?" Annetta said.

"Yeah. Now Reg is gone, we're supposed to do something else with it."

"Move it again?"

"The Men Who Aren't There almost found the billabong in Australia. Whatever they left in that book in Reg's father's handwriting frightened him enough to skip the country. Now they've found it here because he wasn't around to protect it. I think now… it's up to us."

"How are we supposed to put that cat back in the bag?"

"Maybe we don't. Wherever it goes from here, it must eat. Any way we help the bunyip means more people die."

"Why the hell did we get dragged into this mess? To stand here and watch it die?"

I shared Annetta's outrage — but I couldn't play the part of a passive witness. The Men in Black messed with our lives. The Men Who Aren't There threatened to end them. That made us as much a part of this as them and the bunyip. The hilltop provided a clear view of the melee on the bank. Men in Black grappled to gather bunyip eggs. Men Who Aren't There flickered in and out of existence to impede them, block them, even knock the eggs from their hands. The bunyip coiled in the moist earth, lashing with its lethal talons, snapping its powerful tusks. Beyond, sprawled a bowl of earth and rock. Over the hilltop the meadow and the road used by the Men in Black. Everywhere else, sheer walls — impassable, stony inclines — except for the Billabong Trail.

"A billabong is part of a river cut off by erosion," I said.

Annetta raised an eyebrow. "Okay?"

"It becomes an isolated pool, like a grotto, or a cove. There's no regular water source. It remains full as long as the original river water doesn't evaporate. Only rain and flooding replenish it. This billabong is cut off from more than a water source."

"It's cut off from our world," Annetta said. "Except when conditions let one or the other overflow into each other."

"Yeah, and there's only one conduit for it."

"The trail."

"Reg fled Australia when the Men Who Aren't There got too close to finding the trail. On Long Island, after whatever happened to him in

2004, there was no one to keep tabs on them, hide the trail, or move it. They found their way here. Now they'll do whatever frightened Reg enough to schlep himself and a bunyip egg halfway around the world. Annetta, baby, I think we're meant to cut off access to the trail and shut them out forever."

"Won't that cut the bunyip off from its food source and starve it?"

"Maybe. Don't think of it like that. Think of it as saving all the lives it would claim when it feeds. Really, we don't know what will happen to it. Maybe it can eat other things. Maybe it only needs to eat when it reproduces, and it will just live out its days here alone. We ran out of time for research. We know what we know, that's it. Now we have to do something."

"Okay, fine, but, Ben, baby, how the hell do we get home?"

"The trail. We have to be on the other side of the line when we close it."

"That trail comes out somewhere in Australia."

"We could use a vacation, couldn't we?"

Annetta's expression blanked for a moment, then she burst out laughing at the absurdity of our situation, our lack of control over our own destiny, the barrage of practical questions raised by the idea of walking out of this anomalous place into another country, another continent without documentation, or means of getting home, without even a toothbrush, then she yanked me to her and kissed me.

"Next time I get bored with our routine lives," she said, "you sit me down and talk me right out of it, you hear me? You have any idea how to close the trail?"

"Look."

I pointed to a rock wall that rose above the highest point of the trail before it sloped down to the bank of the billabong. A massive, balanced stone perched there like a sleeping falcon.

"We knock that down," I said.

"I know you've been hitting the gym, sweetie, but that's a lot of rock to move by hand."

"We need help, and here's how we get it."

Annetta sighed after I explained my plan, but she didn't protest.

We scurried down the hillside to the billabong then crept toward the melee between the Men in Black and the Men Who Aren't There. They moved in an awkward way, and I couldn't fathom why one or the other group hadn't yet triumphed. They looked slowed down and out of step with time. Like Reg's experience trying to catch up to them but the black car receding as he raced toward it. Annetta and I ducked under the fracas. I grabbed one bunyip egg. Annetta threw a softball-sized stone at the bunyip, striking it above one shimmery eye. It saw us and the egg in my arms. Then we ran.

The bunyip howled and chased us.

We clambered up the rocky hill as fast as we could go, the egg tilting me off balance. The bunyip uncoiled itself and splashed through the billabong. Its howl echoed in the earthen bowl. At the top, I gasped. A stitch ached in my side. The bunyip mounted the hill. I placed the egg near the balanced stone, then Annetta and I backed away. The bunyip surged, grasped the egg in its mouth, then curled and retreated to the billabong. Its powerful body shoved against the stone. Trickles of sand and dirt rattled down into the water.

The melee on the bank halted. The Men in Black gazed up, eyes blacked out by their hat brims.

The stone rocked, seemed about to regain its equilibrium. I ran full speed and threw my whole weight against it. An ear-splitting crack filled the air. It leaned past the point of no return.

"Run!" I shouted.

Annetta and I sprinted down the other side of the hill, sliding, stumbling, skidding in the scree. We hit the overgrown line and kept moving. Figures flicker-flashed past, creating waves of biting cold around us. We poured on all the speed we had. A thunderous crash came, then the rattle and clatter of smaller stones tumbling. I tripped against a buried root or stone. Annetta plowed into me. We fell. We looked back at the trail — gone! Where we'd run was only a drop into the secret water Reg had written of in his manuscript.

Annetta and I helped each other to our feet. Around us sprawled unfamiliar terrain. The high sun of mid-afternoon set us perspiring immediately. We brushed dirt and dust off ourselves. A trail beckoned to us. We followed it and hoped it led to a road, hoped a car or truck with a helpful driver came along.

As we walked, we debated what to say to explain how we wound up in the middle-of-nowhere Australia and settled on two options: claiming amnesia or telling the truth.

Afterword

Some details have been withheld to protect those involved and prevent people – or others – from undoing what Ben and Annetta accomplished. I personally confirmed many facts for myself during my writing.

Ben and Annetta found their way home from Australia, largely due to the help of an Australian cryptozoologist, who read the story of two mysterious travelers in the Sydney Morning Herald. They settled on a combination of truth and obfuscation, admitting to hunting the bunyip, but claiming no memory of traveling to Australia or how they wound up in the Outback. I've since corresponded with the woman, who confirmed many facts, including several too alarming to include in this narrative.

A stop at Riverhead Kayak and Canoe established the loss of the kayaks and Ben's meeting with Officer Nowak. Mr. Owens cajoled fifty dollars out of me for the information. I phoned Officer Nowak, seeking confirmation of his involvement. When I mentioned the Peconic River Monster, he hung up.

I visited the house at 4 Estuary Drive, now a mostly collapsed ruin. The structural damage done years ago caught up with it. Whatever basement nest may have housed the bunyip is now entirely inaccessible, buried under layers of debris. A sinister air hangs about the place. Hair-raising. Uncomfortable. A sense of being observed. At one point during my visit, I thought I'd seen men in the woods along the riverbank, but each time I looked closer, no one was there. Tricks of the light, I hope. A visit to the town clerk's office showed the deed for the house held in an Australian trust with no details as to who controls it.

Gary and Joanna, interviewed by Ben, confirmed their accounts, so long as I agreed not to use their real names.

I contemplated a trip to Australia to hunt the secret campsite and trail of the Burgess family. After several weeks of feeling as if I were never alone and glimpsing inexplicable flashes of motion from the corner of my eye, after seeing outdated black cars with blue-and-gold license plates everywhere I went, I decided against it, deleted all the bookmarks I'd saved for plane tickets, hotels, and a Land Rover rental, and even cleared my cache. The next day all sense of being watched ended. I haven't seen that distinctive black car since.

Lastly, I contacted Malik Campbell. He has not seen nor heard any evidence of Bigfoot or Men in Black since events concluded with the Montauk Monster. At the time of his phone call to Ben, he was on a long-overdue vacation with Janae Campbell. Neither knew anything of the bunyip investigation until they arrived home to find Ben's car in their driveway and their research scattered around their house.

Who are the Men Who Aren't There? What do the Men in Black do with bunyip hatchlings and bunyip eggs? What happened to Reginald Burgess? What happened to his father? Sometimes we're not meant to know all the answers. We glimpse behind the curtain of the universe's inner workings, we learn enough to make a choice, to act, and we hope it all turns out for the best.

Mystery and uncertainty are, always have been, and always will be, an inescapable part of life.

James Chambers
Northport, NY

About the Artist

Although Jason Whitley has worn many creative hats, he is at heart a traditional illustrator and painter. With author James Chambers, Jason collaborates and illustrates the sometimes-prose, sometimes graphic novel, *The Midnight Hour,* which is being collected into one volume by eSpec Books. His and Scott Eckelaert's newspaper comic strip, Sea Urchins, has been collected into four volumes. Along with eSpec Books' Systema Paradoxa series, Jason is working on a crime noir graphic novel. His portrait of Charlotte Hawkins Brown is on display in the Charlotte Hawkins Brown Museum.

artist's rendition of the Bunyip

THE BUNYIP

(Also known as Gu-ru-ngaty, Kianpraty, Banib, Mulyawonk, Yaa-loo, Dongu, Kine Pratie, Wowee-wowee, and Mirree-ulla.)

ORIGINS: Accounts of this fierce creature as a part of the native Australian fauna go back for many centuries, with depictions represented in Aboriginal cave art and purported remains displayed in Australia's museums all the way into the 19th century. It is said to be an aquatic animal living in creeks, swamps, billabongs, riverbeds lakes, and waterholes.

Many of the sightings are from the areas around Victoria, New South Wales, and South Australia, particularly Lake George and the Murray River. Written first-hand reports go back all the way to the mid-1800s.

The Aboriginal nations have at least nine regional variations of the Bunyip, all of them consistent in depicting a menacing aquatic creature with a taste for human flesh. In fact, the word Bunyip is said to translate to "devil" or "evil spirit" in the Wemba-Wemba language.

Some attribute this cryptid solely to Aboriginal folklore and mythology but modern accounts persist.

DESCRIPTION: While the nature of the Bunyip has not varied significantly until the modern day (popular media had taken away its teeth, making it into a shy, but friendly beastie aimed at entertaining children), the Bunyip's physical attributes have always wildly diverged from account to account. It is believed this is, in part, because as a water-dwelling creature few sightings have revealed more than its head and neck, but observers rarely agree even on those features.

There are primarily three head types reported: emu-, dog-, or horse-like. Some claimed crocodile-like, as well. Length varies between four and fifteen feet long, depending on the witness. It is said to range from the size of a dog to the size of a horse.

Other traits cited in the collected reports are one or two eyes, fins, flippers, horns, tusks, dark fur and/or feathers, whiskers, and prominent ears. Some say no tail, others claim it resembles a horse's. They are reported by some to have powerful hind legs on which they walk when they are on dry land, and sharp claws.

While there are other variations, for the sake of brevity, we will stop here, other than to say that two very peculiar descriptions exist that diverge from those more commonly encountered. One extreme variation cites the Bunyip as snake-like, and another claims it is shaped like a giant starfish.

One thing all reports seem to agree on, however, is that the Bunyip is deadly, amphibious, nocturnal, with powerful musk, and a terrifying roar.

LIFE CYCLE: It is said that Bunyip lay massive, pale blue eggs, allegedly in platypus nests. No other details are available.

HISTORY: Many documented reports of Bunyip sightings occurred in the mid-1800s, as naturalists and explorers began cataloging the region and the influx of European settlers increased.

The first use of the word bahnyip was printed in 1812, used to describe a creature roughly fitting accounts of this cryptid. The specific spelling, Bunyip, was first used in 1845. The first newspaper accounts featured discoveries of fossils that, when shown to Aboriginal natives, were identified as Bunyip. These were displayed for many years in the natural history museum.

In 1852, an escaped convict living among the Wathaurong people wrote in his bibliography of several fleeting incidents where he witnessed the Bunyip, though he could not claim to have seen the whole creature.

Similar accounts were documented in 1857 by an artist traveling down the Murray River with his mother. He included sketches of his first-hand sighting of no less than six creatures he identified as Bunyips.

These are just two of many accounts associated with the Bunyip.

Those who wish to rationalize these sightings theorize that the individuals reporting the encounter have confused live sightings with various seals, cassowaries, or crocodiles; and remains with extinct marsupials such as Diprotodon, Zygomaturus, Nototherium, or Palorchestes.

CAPTURE THE CRYPTIDS!

Cryptid Crate is a monthly subscription box filled with various cryptozoology and paranormal themed items to wear, display and collect. Expect a carefully curated box filled with creeptastic pieces from indie makers and artisans pertaining to bigfoot, sasquatch, UFOs, ghosts, and other cryptid and mysterious creatures (apparel, decor, media, etc).

http://CryptidCrate.com

www.ingramcontent.com/pod-product-compliance
Lightning Source LLC
Chambersburg PA
CBHW030807190726
48285CB00003B/1066